THE
MAGPIE'S
LIBRARY

THE MAGPIE'S LIBRARY

KATE BLAIR

DCB

The publisher gratefully acknowledges the support of the Canada Council
for the Arts and the Ontario Arts Council for its publishing program.
We acknowledge the financial support of the Government of Canada through
the Canada Book Fund (CBF) for our publishing activities, and the Government of
Ontario through Ontario Creates, an agency of the Ontario Ministry of Culture,
and the Ontario Book Publishing Tax Credit Program.

LIBRARY AND ARCHIVES CANADA CATALOGUING IN PUBLICATION

Blair, Kate, author
The magpie's library / by Kate Blair.

Issued in print and electronic formats.
ISBN 978-1-77086-554-9 (softcover). — ISBN 978-1-77086-555-6 (HTML)

1. Title.

PS8603.L3153M34 2019   JC813'.6   C2018-906278-9
                                                C2018-906279-7

United States Library of Congress Control Number: 2018967099

Cover illustration and design: Emma Dolan
Interior text design: tannicegdesigns.ca

Printed and bound in Canada.
Printer: Friesens

DCB
AN IMPRINT OF CORMORANT BOOKS INC.
260 SPADINA AVENUE, SUITE 502, TORONTO, ONTARIO, M5T 2E4
www.dcbyoungreaders.com
www.cormorantbooks.com

To my Hayling family —
especially my sister Jo, who taught me to read,
and my Mum, who taught her.

One for sorrow,
Two for mirth
Three for a funeral,
Four for a birth
Five for heaven
Six for hell
Seven's the devil, his own sel'
— Traditional

Chapter One

I'd have noticed something was wrong sooner, if the magpie hadn't distracted me.

It perched on Grandpa's little front lawn, at the end of the cluttered cul-de-sac. I expected it to fly away as we pulled up in front of the small square house. But it tilted its head, the black bead of its eye fixed on us.

The wipers smeared the water back and forth, back and forth.

Mum shivered as she turned off the engine. "One for sorrow."

"Why is the front door open?" Ollie's voice came from the back seat.

I squinted, expecting to see Grandpa, but the entrance to his house was dark and empty.

"He's probably waiting for us," I said. "Standing back so he doesn't get wet."

"That's stupid, Silva. He doesn't know we're coming."

"Shut it, Ollie." After a three-hour drive, I'd hit my limit with my whiny little brother.

But he had a point. Grandpa wouldn't be expecting us on a random Friday in November. The whole thing was weird. Normally, Mum was super fierce about the importance of school, but she'd told our teachers we were sick and dragged us down to Hayling for a surprise visit.

I hadn't complained. I got to spend the drive reading, and I'd been excited to see Grandpa and get away from our mess of a flat. The place was half-packed as we prepared to leave behind yet another city.

"Stop it. Both of you," Mum said. For a moment there was silence, apart from the thrumming of rain on the roof. "That door doesn't shut unless you really slam it. That's probably all it is. Come on."

I stuffed my book into the glove compartment and scurried into the hissing wet, my hand a pointless shield against the driving rain.

In the front hall, Mum's concerned frown was caught in the gold-framed mirror. She ran a hand through her wet pixie-cut. My own hair was plastered against my head and shoulders, chilly on the bare skin of my neck. Ollie joined us, shaking his unkempt hair like a dog.

"Dad?" Mum called.

"Maybe he popped out," I said.

"In this rain?" Ollie asked. "And what about the post?"

Envelopes were strewn across the carpet, the nearest ones soggy. For a ridiculous moment I wondered if we were in the wrong house. But Grandpa's battered boots sat in the hall, waiting for his feet to fill them.

I swallowed at the wrongness of it. He always kept the house tidy and, other than getting a tad forgetful, he never changed. He was always here to greet us. He always gave me Jelly Babies when we'd visit, because they'd been my favorite when I was small. He'd taught me to bite the heads off first, "so they didn't suffer." And it didn't matter that I was thirteen, I'd always be his little girl.

A chill slunk into my gut, cooling the excitement that had warmed me in the car.

"I thought Chloe was cleaning for him," Mum said. Chloe was my second cousin. She lived next door with her mum, Janet.

"Then Chloe's doing a rubbish job," Ollie said.

I crept into the front room. A plate with a moldy crumpet sat on the coffee table. The fire was unlit, the room cold.

"Perhaps I should check on my own," Mum said. "You two can wait outside."

"Fine. I'll be in the car." Ollie stomped out.

I wanted to escape too, but I had to know if Grandpa was okay.

In the kitchen, filthy dishes spilled out of the sink and across the countertop. All-Bran littered the floor like playground woodchips. It was as if the neat façade of Grandpa's home had crumbled, revealing a mess of maggots at the core.

I ran upstairs.

"Grandpa?" I kept my voice cheerful, and headed to the end of the corridor, to the room I stayed in during the school holidays.

That at least looked normal: a cozy space tucked under the eaves with bookshelves filling all available wall space. I felt a superstitious desire to check the old wardrobe, like I checked all wardrobes when I was younger, even the IKEA ones in our rented flats, searching for Narnia.

It was empty, aside from skeletal hangers and a cardigan I'd been looking for since the summer. What had I expected? That Grandpa would be hiding in here, or that I'd be looking into a winter wonderland?

The creak and bang of doors opening and closing came from down the hall as Mum checked the other rooms.

Something brushed against my leg. I leapt back, but it was Gin, one of Janet's cats, purring as she rubbed against me, tail high. I stroked her. Wet fur stuck to my hand. I wiped it on my jeans as a lump grew in my stomach.

Mum had gone quiet. I hurried out into the hall where she stood, looking lost.

"I'll see if Janet knows anything." As she dialed, I tried to give her a reassuring smile.

"It's me. I'm at Dad's house, but ..." She turned away abruptly. "When?" A long pause. "All right. We'll head straight there."

Mum hung up, and gripped the bannister. "Janet came

by earlier and found Grandpa on the floor. They're at the hospital."

We hurried back out to the car. Ollie was slumped in the back seat, legs spread, staring at his phone. He didn't bother looking up as we clambered in, and Mum turned the engine on.

The magpie still perched on the lawn. It watched us as we drove away.

The girl and her mother dashed through the rain to a small red car. None but the girl saw me as they backed out of the drive, turning the corner too fast. Her wide eyes remained fixed upon me until they were gone. But even she only saw a normal black-and-white bird.

Emotion trailed behind them, like fog hung upon the air: fear, worry, isolation. Yet I saw through it, beheld the glitter beneath; the enticing shine emitted by all lonely souls.

Follow them, The Whisper said.

I took to the sky, wheeling on wings as black as a hole in the world. The car joined the thread of traffic; other people, separated from each other in their colorful tin carriages. I let the sea air buoy me, sharp and salty.

I saw it all: the village, the island, the world. People cocooned within their own little lonelinesses: cars, head-phones, and screens. The silences and spaces between them stretched until they swallowed them whole.

The cars shrank to the size of toys as I rose. I could still feel the right one, its metal red as a bead of blood; I could feel the ache inside. But they crossed the bridge and joined the rush of cars upon the motorway. I could not keep up. There was too much traffic: a torrent of emotion.

I lost the girl and her family.

You will find them again, The Whisper said. *I shall help you find those who need you. Together, we can offer them comfort. Together we can hold them tight. Together we keep them safe, sealed in your collection.*

Forever.

Chapter Two

In the ward, six beds hid behind curtains, three on either side. We traipsed through the antiseptic stink, wet shoes squeaking on the floor, past the murmurs and moans of unseen patients.

The low rumble of Grandpa's voice came from the farthest bed. Relief shot through me. I ran the last few yards and yanked the fabric aside with a clatter of curtain rings.

"Grandpa!"

He lay beneath the sheets, brow furrowed. A tube looped from his hand to an IV bag. Janet, Mum's cousin, stood next to him, wearing too much makeup and a brittle smile.

The second Grandpa saw Mum, his familiar grin spread across his face, almost too wide to fit. "Ruthie, thank goodness you're here."

We stared at him. Ruth was my grandmother. She'd died when Mum was a teen.

Mum's voice wavered as she spoke. "It's me, Dad. Liz. Your ... daughter."

Grandpa's hazel eyes clouded with confusion. How could he not know her?

"Silva! Oliver!" Janet prompted him. "Lovely to see you."

Grandpa struggled to sit up, revealing a short-sleeved hospital gown and the old-fashioned doll tattoo on his upper arm. "You have to get me out of here."

Janet pulled the blanket back over Grandpa's chest. "Don't worry, Uncle Chris."

"Grandpa, are you okay?" I knew it was a stupid question.

His gaze fell on me, suspicion simmering behind it. Something inside me crumpled.

"It's me, Silva." I wanted him to stop it, to be himself again. I wanted to climb onto the bed and hug him, to breathe in his biscuits-and-aftershave smell. But he twisted toward Mum, wincing as he moved.

"Take me home, Ruthie."

I grabbed the metal bar at the end of the bed to steady myself.

"I'm going to the loo," Ollie said.

"Ollie …" Mum started, but he hurried away.

Grandpa's eyes darted around. "You know I hate hospitals."

His words distorted in my ears. I couldn't deal with the look he'd given me, as if I'd been erased from his life.

"The doctor is doing her rounds now," Janet said. "She thinks it's an infection and dehydration. Making him worse than normal."

Worse than normal. What did that mean?

"He needs fluids and antibiotics and will be in for a few days. I'll get Chloe to clean the house." Janet nodded at Grandpa. "He fired her."

"You fired Chloe?" Mum asked.

"He was acting so strangely. That's why I messaged you."

Grandpa yanked on Mum's wrist. Pulled her close. "Don't let them keep me here."

"I'll speak to the doctor, Dad. See what she says."

An uncomfortable silence spread like a swamp between us. After what felt like a long time, Mum spoke. "Silva, could you check and see if Ollie is okay?"

I nodded and reeled away. As I passed another set of curtains, I glimpsed the scene inside through the small gap. A white sheet lay over a still body. A woman sat beside the bed, head in her hands. I looked away fast, like death could be catching, and I could carry it back to Grandpa.

In the wide hallway, beds and equipment lined the walls, as though washed there by a flood. People drifted down the corridors, clutching tissues and iv poles tight as life preservers.

I found Ollie slumped on a wheelchair, staring at his phone. His eyes were dry. Mum needn't have worried.

He was fine. He'd just wanted to play one of his stupid apps.

Irritation filled me with heat. It would be nice not to care, like Ollie. Whenever we moved to a new town, he didn't need to try to fit in. Life was easy for him. He played football: FIFA games on his phone and the real thing at school, and ended up with a ton of friends.

"Someone might need that." I kicked the tire of the wheelchair.

"I'll move if they ask," Ollie said.

There was a slope down the hall. I fought the urge to shove the wheelchair down it.

"I thought you were going to the loo."

"Just been," he said.

"Then we should go back. Don't you care about Grandpa?"

Ollie's jaw clenched, although he still didn't look up. I grabbed his arm, and yanked him to his feet. "Stop being so selfish."

"Ow." His trainers squeaked as he dragged his feet.

When we got back to the ward, it was clear the doctor had come and gone. Mum and Janet faced off over Grandpa's bed.

Mum turned to us. "We've got to get the house ready. Dad's coming home tomorrow."

"Tomorrow?" I asked. "I thought the doctor said he had to stay."

"She did," Janet said.

"They'd like to keep him in longer," Mum said. "But if there's an improvement from the antibiotics, we can take him home. He'll recover faster where he feels safe."

Janet folded her arms. "The doctor said this is a serious infection. You're putting his life at risk, and you'll dash off again."

"Just … leave it, Janet." Mum's jaw was set.

"We've got school," I pointed out.

"It's only a couple of weeks until we move to Manchester. We need to take care of your grandfather."

"Wouldn't the hospital be better for that?" Ollie said.

For once, I agreed with him.

Mum pinched the bridge of her nose. "Look. Let's get in the car. There's something I should have told you two. Something we should talk about in private."

Mum gave Grandpa a quick kiss, and hurried us off the ward. His fragile gaze and Janet's disapproving glare followed us until they disappeared behind the curtains.

The rain eased off, replaced by a drizzle that streaked the windscreen as the wipers swung back and forth. We drove in silence out of the car park. Mum was quiet so long I jumped when she started talking.

"Janet called yesterday because she was worried about Grandpa. But you know how she exaggerates things, so I phoned. When he didn't answer, I decided to check."

"Why didn't you just tell us?" I asked.

"I didn't want to worry you. You may have noticed he's been a bit forgetful lately."

"Only stuff like where he'd put the remote. He wasn't forgetting me."

A lorry sliced through a puddle beside us, splattering our windscreen. Mum turned the wipers up. Thwap. Thwap. Thwap.

"He had tests done a couple of months ago. He has Alzheimer's."

My ears rang. "Alzheimer's?"

"Yes. It's a kind of dementia. A slow loss of memory."

"That's why he didn't recognize me?"

"Yes. I'm afraid it's going to get worse. He'll forget more and more over time. There's no cure, but he probably has years left."

"It's going to kill him?"

"Not for a very long time."

I glanced in the rearview mirror, expecting to see Ollie on his phone. But he stared out of the window as we crossed the bridge to the island, the choppy gray water of high tide beneath us.

"That wasn't a slow loss of memory," I pointed out.

"Right now, the infection is making him much more confused." Mum flexed her fingers, then gripped the wheel again. "Antibiotics will help get him back to normal."

"Janet said you're putting his life at risk."

Mum was silent for a long moment. The tires hissed

on the curves of the road. Thatched houses dripped like damp dogs as we passed.

"It's all about balance. And what life he has left."

That chilled me to the core. The wipers swished back and forth. Thwap. Thwap. Thwap.

"You're going to let him die."

"No," Mum said, fast and firm. "Not *let* him die. We'll do everything in our power to get him through this infection."

"But —"

"He's 80. We can't keep him alive forever. He hates hospitals."

"We can't just give up."

"No one is giving up, Silva." But Mum's voice was resigned.

I leaned my forehead against the cold window. We had to do something. Had to find a way to make this better. I wanted to look up Alzheimer's on my phone and see what treatments there were, but I was out of data. Grandpa didn't have Wi-Fi, just a plug-in connection that didn't work with my mobile.

Ahead of us rose the familiar peaked shape of Hayling Library, like an island in the sodden green. Another magpie perched on the wall outside: two for joy. Wasn't that how that old rhyme went? Maybe it was a sign. It was a better idea than going back to the mess of Grandpa's house, anyway. Plus, the library had Wi-Fi.

"Can I go to the library?"

Mum raised an eyebrow, but flipped on the indicator and turned into the car park. "I guess you could pick up some books. I can get started on cleaning." Mum tugged on the handbrake and rummaged in her purse. She held out a £20 note. "Grab some fish and chips for us on the way home. The kitchen's in a right state. Ollie, are you going with Silva?"

Ollie glanced up. I was tempted to ask him to come. There was only a year between our ages, and when we were little, we'd sit on the train in the children's section, reading books together. I missed the old Ollie, the boy behind the phone. But a voice in my head told me it was pointless. Even if he came, he'd only sulk. I hadn't been like that, even at twelve. Of course, I hadn't been allowed a phone until I was thirteen, and then Ollie was given one at the exact same time. He always had it easier than I did.

Ollie gave one shake of his head. No surprise there. I clambered out of the car and dashed through the drizzle.

Inside the library, the patter of the rain stilled, replaced by an echoing quiet, broken only by the occasional cough of an old woman browsing in the military history section. My soggy jeans clung to my legs like wet plaster.

The wooden ceiling rose to a point, supported by a star of white girders, strip lights dangling from them. I took a moment to breathe in the familiar floor-polish smell.

At the desk at the back sat a dark-skinned woman in a purple dress. "Hi there." She wasn't shouting, but her

Portsmouth accent carried. "Is it lunchtime at the school?"

"I don't go there. I'm visiting family. I have a library card." I pulled it out of my jacket pocket and held it up, like a bus pass.

Her brow furrowed. "Didn't I see you here in the summer?"

"Probably. I was here a lot. I'm Silva."

"I'm Asha. You were reading *The Dark is Rising*, right? It's one of my favorites."

"Mine too."

Her grin widened. "Oh! Then I have so many recommendations for you."

"I just wanted to use the Wi-Fi. I need to look up stuff on … on Alzheimer's." Tears pricked at my eyes. I wiped at them, quickly.

"Oh. I see." Her smile vanished. "It's not for a school project, I'm guessing."

I shook my head.

"I'm so sorry to hear it. Connect away. Why don't you sit down at one of the tables and I'll see if I can find some books, too."

I sat down, signed into the library's Wi-Fi, and searched. I found an article on celebrities raising money for Alzheimer's charities, another about spotting the first symptoms, and a third on keeping your brain active. None of it was helpful. Asha's footsteps echoed through the library. She came over with two books and a concerned expression.

"I'm afraid it's heavy stuff. If you need any help under-
standing it, or just want to talk, let me know. All right?"

"Thanks." I flipped open the first book.

Half an hour later I was numb.

I read fast, but the books were tough to follow in places.
What I understood was bleak. At his age, Grandpa might
have five or more years of life left, but he'd forget all
of us. He'd lose his personality, his ability to walk, and
slowly die.

On the page in front of me was a photo of a slice of
post-mortem brain. Someone's memories, their life, cut
open and stuck to the page. I slammed the book closed
and shoved it away. I got up and headed for the shelves.

I wandered up and down, pulling out a few of my
favorites: *A Wrinkle in Time*, *The Night Circus*, and
Harry Potter. The first Harry Potter, as everything was
okay at the end of that one, and I needed a happy ending.

Because in real life, I wasn't going to get one.

I hugged them against my chest as I drifted to my table.
I tried to slip into the stories. They were usually my life-
line, my escape from moving between suburbs and small
towns, between bland flats and rented houses. They were
my camouflage. I could sit reading, and I was invisible.
Being the invisible girl was better than being the new
girl. When you're the new girl you don't know if people
are being nice or sarcastic, until you're surrounded by
mocking laughter.

But I couldn't concentrate. Grandpa was dying. He didn't recognize me. Without him, what was there? I faded in and out of schools too fast to have anyone remember me. Mum was submerged in a job that moved us from town to town so fast I never knew my own postcode. Ollie didn't think about anything other than himself.

If Grandpa didn't remember me, it would be as if I didn't exist at all.

That's when I saw it: a flash of shining blue-black with a hint of white. It swooped down from the high windows to the floor, and landed between two shelves in front of me.

A magpie.

How had it got inside? Was there a window open in this weather? It hopped forwards, cocked its head sideways with that odd jerking motion birds have.

I glanced over at Asha to see if she'd noticed, but she was poking at her keyboard with one finger, nose crinkled, as if her computer had insulted her.

The bird bobbed onward. It twitched its neck around, dark eye on me. I had this odd feeling it wanted me to follow. It resumed its skittish hops. I stood and trailed behind it, feeling a bit silly. I followed it down a corridor of biographies, all the way to the pink-and-white spines of the romances. When I reached the back of the library, it vanished.

But there was an arched door: a wooden door, far

too old for the modern building, with the silhouette of a magpie singed into it.

It was like something from the middle ages, squeezing itself into a space that should have been a blank wall. The wood was thick and pock-marked with age. My fingertips brushed against the ancient timber. It felt real. Felt as solid as the shelves, the books, the regular library. I laid my palm against it, felt the dry grain, the hard knots. It looked heavy.

And yet, when I pushed, it swung open easily.

Chapter Three

The door opened with a soft creak, revealing a round room, an impossible room. Warm air wafted out, with the comforting old-book smell of vanilla and stale coffee. Roots ran across the dark marble floor and branches climbed the stone walls, but instead of leaves, hundreds of colorful books balanced on the uneven limbs.

My hand went to my mouth. I stepped into the room and the door closed quietly behind me. Sunlight shone through a glass dome, filling the air with the glitter of dust motes, floating like miniature fireflies.

A mahogany chair stood in the center of the room. The magpie perched on it, the black of its wings contrasted against the red-brown wood. There was no one else in the room. Still, I turned around, just to check.

The only door was the one I'd come through. Could I get back? I darted over and opened it. There were the metal shelves of Hayling Library, gray and dull.

I let out a breath. I could leave now. Return, but to what? The books about Alzheimer's? Grandpa's mess of a house? His blank expression when he looked at me?

I let the door to the normal world swing shut again.

Six roots sprouted from the floor under the old chair in the middle of the magical library, cutting the circular room into sections like a wheel. They forked as they reached the walls and climbed up, splitting and branching, standing proud of the stone, countless books budding from their multiplying limbs like vibrant leaves: a busy smatter of color against the dark stone. The roots and branches made the library feel like a burrow, a forest, or a nest of shelves.

I used to dream of finding somewhere like this, but I'd given up long ago. I'd got no letter from Hogwarts. When we'd briefly lived in Oxford, I'd searched among the hornbeam trees of the northern ring road for Cittàgazze, and found nothing but the litter tossed from car windows.

But this was a real magical library. And it was mine. The first thing in forever that was really mine. This library was beautiful. Inexplicable. Everything I'd dreamed of.

But it didn't change anything. Grandpa was still dying.

The magpie watched as I approached the chair in the center of the room. A cushion softened the seat, embroidered with a tapestry of leaves. It was clearly the heart of the room, inviting me to sit and read.

"What is this place?" I asked the magpie.

It took off, flying so close that the breeze from its wings grazed my cheek. It fluttered up to a small, empty shelf near the top of the library, and perched there. I wandered over, alongside one of the six roots as it snaked across the dark ground.

"Am I meant to read a story?" It sounded stupid when I said it out loud. But the magpie tilted its head forward twice: a pecking motion, or a nod.

I spun on the spot, and the books blurred around me. "Which one?"

The magpie's wings rustled in a quick bunching movement, like a shrug.

One of the roots reached the bottom of the wall in front of me. There was only one book on the lowest shelf. I bent down and picked it up. It was ancient, and bound in leather. The front was embossed with an image of a girl. She wore a big dress like one of Henry VIII's wives and I knew enough from school and books set in the past, and Grandpa taking us to see the remains of the Mary Rose at the Historic Dockyards in Portsmouth years ago, that this had to be from about the sixteenth century. I eased it open. Thick italic letters covered the paper, handwritten. I tried to make out the words, but the letters were too pointy, too crowded.

"I can't read this."

Again, the magpie gave that odd shrug of its wings.

Fragments of old ink flaked off the thick paper. I closed it gently, afraid I'd damaged it. This book was probably nearly five hundred years old. It should be read with gloves, by an expert. I slid it back onto its shelf.

"Sorry," I said.

The stories around it were almost as ancient, so I let my fingers trace along the shining shelves as they snaked their way up the wall. The books got newer as the branches forked and climbed. They faded from the dark brown of leather into deep red bindings, pastel hardbacks, then paperbacks with glossy spines. The uppermost shelves held books that would have looked at home in a modern bookstore, except the spines were blank: no titles, no author names.

I stood on tiptoe to grab the highest book I could reach. On the cover was a teen with slicked-back hair and a leather jacket. He leaned on a jukebox, peering down through the brightly lit glass at the stacked records. No title or author on the front. I flipped it over. There was nothing on the back, either.

Inside, the story started at the top of the first sheet. I flicked forward, looking for chapters breaks or illustrations, but there was nothing but text. Not far in, it cut off halfway down a page, leaving the rest of the sheets blank.

As I closed the book, a movement on the page caught my eye; a small scurrying, like an insect. But when I opened it again, everything was still. I shivered.

I slid it back on its shelf, and picked another. On this one was a younger boy, in a hall of mirrors, wearing a cap and short trousers. The reflections were distorted, but they weren't his. They were other children and teens, in clothes from different ages.

"Books usually have descriptions on the back to tell you what they're about. These don't say anything. How am I meant to choose?"

Another little wing shrug.

"I'm … not good at decisions right now. I just got bad news about my Grandpa."

The magpie nodded and hopped to a different branch. It turned its gaze onto a book. A rustle came from the shelf. The book sitting on it slid out, inch by inch, until it reached the edge. I held my hands out to catch it, afraid it would tip and fall. But the book opened and spread its pages as if they were wings. I froze, open-mouthed as it flew around the room, bobbing up and down as the cover flapped. It spun and wheeled, doing one more graceful circuit of the library before gliding down to where I stood.

It landed gently on my palms, cover-side up.

It was a hardback, with a pastel painting of a teen girl in a white nightgown. She knelt on the floor of a white room. I saw what she was clutching, and there was a suspended moment, weightless as the golden motes sparkling in the air around me.

It was an old-fashioned doll, just like the one on Grandpa's arm, with black eyes and ringlets. I hugged the book to my chest.

"My grandpa has a tattoo just like that! Is this book something to do with him?"

The magpie bobbed its head in another nod.

I carried it to the big wooden chair and sat. I opened it at a random point near the end, to see what it was about.

Margaret heard crying, in the next room, breathless and weak, from the younger girl who had just arrived.

The ink seemed deeper than ordinary print. Blacker, with a hint of blue. I ran a hand over the raised letters, fingertips tracing the bumps and gaps.

Something twitched on my thumb. For a moment, I thought it was an insect, but it looked more like the letter "M." It moved across my skin, bunching up and stretching like a caterpillar. I froze as it inched across my hand.

Other letters were moving, too, crawling off the page, and I realized, in the old book, the first book I'd picked up, it hadn't been the ink "flaking" off the paper. The letters had been climbing from their places on the pages, just like here. Words scuttled onto my hands like spiders. I was too shocked to move.

She tried to block it out. Tried not to let the loneliness touch her.

I kept utterly still. Should I swat at them? What if they bit, or stung? The words I'd just read flowed over the backs of my hands, scampered up my arms. But they didn't hurt. They barely tickled.

It wouldn't be long until lights out. Then she'd be alone. Then she could escape.

Sentences crowded onto me like dark lace, until my

hands and arms were covered. The letters left the pages blank. The sheets trembled and rippled, more like milk than paper.

The text tightened around my arms. There was a tug.

Before I could cry out, I was yanked forward, through the surface of the paper, and into the book itself.

I woke in bed. For one wonderful moment, I thought the library and Grandpa's sickness were a dream. But the walls were white, not the bland cream of the rented flats we lived in, and they were bare, punctuated only with a plain calendar, open to February 1946. Half the days were crossed off in thick black pen. A naked light bulb lit the room and a coarse gray blanket covered my legs. In one arm, I clutched a doll with ringlets, black eyes, and a red dress, just like the tattoo on Grandpa's arm.

I felt dizzy. My lungs ached. The smell of bleach surrounded me.

I wished I could be back in my dear room at home, instead of this dreary one at the sanatorium. I was sick of this place, sick of this beastly disease.

Those weren't my thoughts. They were someone else's pushing in on my own, muddling them, making it hard to focus. My body felt strange: my whole being filled with a blood-deep sickness. And it was too skinny, too pale, to be mine.

Not long now. Almost time.

I tried to shake my head to clear the intrusive voice, but

I couldn't move. I tried to speak, but my lips remained shut. That's when it hit me. This wasn't just someone else's room; this was someone else's body. I was in someone else's body, feeling through their skin, wearing their white nightgown.

The hours dragged here, seemed to stretch out for days.

I was the teen girl on the cover of the book: Margaret. I hadn't just been dragged into her story, I'd *become* her. I was in the book, living it through her.

I felt it all: the prickle of the cold air on her skin, making the hairs on her arms stand on end; the catch of breath in her throat, too shallow. I wished she would inhale properly, deeply, or at least cough to clear her lungs.

Soon, I could take a break. Escape this ghastly feeling, this awful sickness.

I should have been scared, but it was thrilling, being in a story. My excitement and Margaret's merged. She clutched the blankets tight as our thoughts intertwined. Her anticipation consumed me, along with the bone-deep ache in her body.

In just a wink, I'd feel whole again. I'd escape from the dreadful loneliness of this hospital with its dashed insistence on rest, rest, endless rest, and more damned rest.

Margaret's hands were porcelain pale. I wanted to look closer. Could I move her body? I concentrated, and tried to lift a hand. I willed myself into Margaret's muscles, her arm, and her wrist. I thought of her body as my own and focused on taking control.

The crying from the next room cut off and Margaret's hand rose.

It was oddly smooth, and heavy. But moving her hand felt wrong, like driving a corpse. Nausea rushed through me, along with a guilty feeling, as if I were breaking an important rule. I let go. The sobbing from the next room restarted, like a radio turning on, and Margaret's hand fell back into place.

Okay, I wasn't allowed to play puppet master. I was just along for the ride. This was Margaret's book; I was an observer in the character's body.

What could be taking Matron so long? It had to be lights out by now!

I was allowed to experience the story, not change it.

And wasn't this exactly what I'd been seeking when I picked out my favorite books in Hayling Library? A chance to slip into a story so completely I forgot my worries.

I stopped fighting to keep hold of my memories. It was a relief to let Margaret's feelings push mine out of the way, a relief to lose myself. I let myself be carried away by her story.

I became Margaret.

Crying came from the next room, breathless and weak, from that young girl who arrived today, still calling for her Mama. I drew in a shaky breath. The sound of weeping was constant here. Patients grieving friends they'd lost, and our own lives, slipping away in the ghastly boredom. I clutched my doll tighter. Soon, I could leave the sanatorium. I could feel like myself again.

There was a knock on the door. It opened and Matron entered, frizzy hair protruding from her starched white cap.

"Lights out?" I said, hopefully.

"A visitor for you. It's out of usual hours, but he said he'd come a long way." She leaned forward. "And he threatened to cry if I said no. Don't tell the doctor, but he can stay for five minutes."

"Thank you," I said, but my stomach sank.

A boy burst past Matron, and into my room, a blur of speed. His short trousers were splattered with mud: my dear little brother.

Matron backed out, closing the door behind her.

"Peggy!" he said, coming over to the bed.

I lifted a heavy arm and ruffled his hair. "Oh, dear heart. What are you doing here? Where are Mama and Papa?"

"They're busy with the brat."

"Do they know you're here?" No answer. "Did you cycle all the way without telling them?"

The crying came louder from the next room. I wanted to cover my brother's ears. He was so full of life. The sanatorium had leached that out of me.

My brother leaned in, toward my bed. "I can get you out of here. Jack's brother's got a motorbike with a sidecar and he knows where the keys are. We could be out of here in a jiffy —"

"Oh, I wish I could. But they'd just bring me back."

My brother's head dropped. "You're getting so weak, Peg. This place is bad for you."

For a moment, I considered telling him about the fun I'd been having among the dolls. But he'd think I was going barmy, locked up here.

"I'm sorry. I've been a terrible drip. Not resting as much as I should. I'll try harder."

He looked up at me with his big eyes. "You'll rest properly? Do everything you can to get out of here? Cross your heart?"

"Cross my heart." I traced my fingers in an "x" and held out a hand for him to shake.

As my brother touched me, his expression froze. "Your hand's cold, Peg. And stiff."

I pulled my arm away and tucked it under the covers. "It's jolly chilly in here at night. They leave the windows open. Fresh air is good for us."

Matron peered in. "Sorry. It's lights out, and they'll have my skin if they catch you here."

"Bye, Peg." My brother dragged his feet as he headed to the door. "Remember your promise. Rest. Get better. Come home."

"I love you," I said. "Tell Mama, Papa, and the baby I love them too."

My brother disappeared through the door. As he left, Matron flicked off the light, leaving me in the dim room.

How I wished I could jump in the sidecar of a motorbike with my darling little brother, wished that we might screech our way out of here, hair in the wind. But it was awful to think like that. It made the sorrow cut deeper; down to my bones.

There was only one place I felt fully myself now. Only one place where I could be well.

I waited for the click of Matron's heels and the squeak of my brother's plimsolls to fade.

My dollhouse stood against the wall, the one thing I was allowed from home.

I'd visit one more time, then have a few nights off. Get more shut-eye. That wasn't breaking my promise. Not really. I was just postponing it for a night.

I put my doll to one side, and struggled to get off the bed. I was shaky and breathless, and my heart beat hard. But I was down, knees aching, on the bitterly cold floor, joints almost locked.

Surely that wasn't normal with tuberculosis, was it?

No matter. I was practically there. I crawled closer to the dollhouse.

The tiny front door didn't fit the toy home. It had been a plain white door before I got sick. But on the most awful night I'd ever known, the sweet little magpie had appeared and with it, the ancient-looking door, a dark bird burned into the wood.

I reached for it, prodded it open with a finger. I felt my hand changing. I felt myself shrinking, with a shiver of relief. I was pulled down, pulled through the door.

I stood in the wood-paneled foyer of the dollhouse and

exhaled. I was me, fully me without that horrible sense of dislocation, that bone-deep pining to be here. Of course, the tuberculosis still held my lungs tight, but the dolls would bring me relief from that.

A twisted tree trunk grew out from the center of the large entrance hall. Wooden steps circled around it with branches for banisters, forming a spiral staircase that looked as if it had grown there. The magpie perched at the top, high above me. I felt weary just looking up there, but most of the dolls on this floor were sick, like me. I began to climb.

It took a long time to get up the first flight. Step, breathe. Step, breathe. I kept going, up to the second, then a bothersome coughing fit hit. I clutched the branch to my side until it passed. My lungs were raw, my legs shaky.

I made it to the third floor, but had to stop on the landing for a long time, leaning against the wall, choking and gasping. When I took my hand from my mouth, I got a nasty jolt.

It was wet with blood.

The magpie looked down on me, something like concern in its dark eyes.

I should be resting, like I'd promised my brother, not climbing staircases. I should go back to bed. I peered down, at the ground floor. A few dolls stood there, clustered around the bottom of the staircase. That was peculiar.

Had they done that before? Left their rooms and gathered there, between me and the front door? I wondered if they'd stop me leaving, and shivered.

No. I was being preposterous. The dolls were helpful, weren't they?

I floundered on. The landing opened into six hallways. I picked the nearest. I peered into the first room. It had plain walls, like a cell, with a figure standing in the middle: a human-sized doll. Or rather, it was me that was doll-sized, shrunk to fit the house. The doll stared straight ahead, skinny frame draped in rags, hair lanky, face spotted with angry red sores.

No. She was sick. The whole point of being here was to feel well. I moved on. The next room was furnished, and covered in dark green wallpaper. The doll in the center wore an extravagant maroon Victorian gown, jewels sparkling on the peachy skin of her neck.

My footsteps were hushed by the soft carpet as I approached. The doll's arms were plump, her cheeks rounded and apple-red, lips a perfect pink bow: the very picture of health.

Yes. My seventh doll. This one.

I reached toward her. The doll lifted her arm, mirroring me. Her hand was warm as it touched my fingertips. I fell forward, into her merciful embrace.

I opened my eyes. Dust glittered in the golden light from the dome above me. The wooden seat was hard against my back, and the book lay on my lap. I stretched, and my arms moved, effortlessly. They were mine again.

It was like waking from a dream, still clasping at the memories of being Margaret, of the sinister dollhouse, but her exhaustion had lifted, and I felt as light as a balloon.

I took a deep breath. The oxygen reached deep into my lungs. It felt good to breathe easily, to not have tuberculosis. I ran my hands over my body, feeling the tingle across my skin, glad to have myself back.

This place was a world of stories. A tree growing novels, branches unfurling leafy pages, adventures for me to enter. Were they all creepy like Margaret's? Or were there fantasies and fairy tales?

The magpie still sat on the top shelf.

I shook my head. "How did ..."

The magpie swooped to land on the arm of my chair, so close that I fought the urge to reach out, to stroke the blue-black sheen of its feathers, the pure white of its chest.

"That was amazing!" I said.

The bird gave a little bow.

"But ... what did it have to do with Grandpa? Was it just the doll tattoo?"

The magpie hopped forward, pointing its beak at the book in my lap.

"You want me to read more? From the beginning?"

A quick nod.

I picked up the story, but as I did, my hands brushed against my jeans: my dry jeans. Cold crept up my back.

"I was soaked when I came in. How long have I been here?"

The bird twitched its head insistently toward Margaret's book.

I pulled out my phone: 4:02 p.m. Over three hours had passed. Mum would be waiting for me, along with the food I'd promised to buy.

I stood. The book slid onto the ground with a thump. The magpie fluttered away, startled.

"Sorry!" I picked up the book, straightened the dust jacket and placed it carefully on the cushion. "I have to go."

The magpie shook its head.

"But I'll come back. I mean, can ... can I come back?"

It nodded, three times, enthusiastically.

"Thank you! I'll be back as soon as I can. I promise!"

I hurried toward the door to the real world and, with a regretful glance at the beautiful library and the magpie sitting in the middle, stepped out.

As soon as the door closed behind me, I worried I'd made a mistake. I spun around, afraid the entrance might have disappeared as inexplicably as it had appeared. But it was still there. I laid my palm on the old wood, on the black magpie singed into it.

A feeling nagged at me, like I'd forgotten something. I almost opened the door again to look for it. But an irregular squeaking made me turn.

Asha pushed a trolley of books past the end of the

aisle. One of the wheels wobbled, squealing as it moved. "Silva! Back for your coat? I stuck it behind the desk. I'll grab it."

My hand was still on the door, but she didn't comment on it. Maybe that's what I'd forgotten: my coat. But that didn't feel right.

Asha reappeared, bounding down the aisle with my jacket over her arm. "I was worried about you. You must have been distracted to go out in the rain without this."

She wasn't looking at the door at all.

"Have you … seen anything strange around here?" I asked.

"Like what?"

"Um … like a magpie?"

"Where?"

That confirmed it. Only I could see the door. "I guess it flew away."

Asha's gaze was tight with concern. "Are you okay?"

"Yeah, I suppose so. Thanks."

"Do you want me to call someone for you?"

"No, no, I'm fine." I stuck a smile on to prove it. "I'll see you soon, all right?"

"Okay," Asha said, although she didn't sound sure.

I stumbled outside, trying to put my whirling thoughts into order. My headache pounded. The rain had steadied to a wet haze that left tiny drops on my phone's screen. I wiped them with my sleeve. A message buzzed in from Mum, asking when I'd be back. I typed a quick reply.

Sorry. Lost track of time. Coming back now.

Asha had put away my coat. The library wasn't big; if I were there, she'd have seen me. And my jeans had dried, so I hadn't gone outside. But I'd gone somewhere for three hours.

I'd actually entered a magical library, and lived through a story.

In my library the girl, Silva, had gone, but a cloud of glittering motes marked where she had sat to read: a trail of shining life she had shed; a piece of her to look after.

Now, keep her safe, said The Whisper.

I flew to the empty shelf. The space upon the branch shimmered, like the air above a hearth. A blank book revealed itself, rustled, and opened. The scraps of light glittered, drifting across the library and into the book. They settled upon the empty pages, and their golden glow faded to the lifeless black of ink. The book closed, sealing them in.

An image developed upon the cover, growing slowly clearer, like the hills when the mists lifted. A picture of Silva, reaching for a book in the library, her face bright with hope.

I missed her already. I would have touched the picture, if I were still a boy. Some never returned. Some were afraid, yet she had seemed enchanted.

I shall help you to bring her back, The Whisper said.

What would I do if I did not have The Whisper? I was not able to recall a time when it had not been close, its velvet voice within my head. Yet, I did not know it as The Whisper at first. It was so quiet that I believed its words were my own thoughts.

The Whisper found me almost five hundred years ago. I was just a baby, left alone after my mother died in childbed. I was the youngest of seven children, and The Whisper told me I was so weak I would not have lived, if it had not been there to keep me company.

But I survived, though I was much afflicted with chin-cough and agues, green sickness and gripings of the belly. The doctors said I must be purged of evil humors, with leeches, cold whey, and bitter herbs. I was kept from my siblings and Father hired a servant, Lettie, to take care of me. For a time, I believed she loved me as if I were her own.

I learned the hard way that I was mistaken. It was my gift that drove her away: the curious little talent that had always been a part of me, a magic The Whisper said was because my mother was the seventh born in her family, and I was her seventh child. Such a birthright made me a blessed child, a special child. But at first, it was only the slightest things I could move with the power within my mind, like the rushes upon our floor. I could make them dance with a thought, as if a miniature tempest gusted among them.

The Whisper showed me how to pull, how to push, how to tilt my thoughts just so and let things come to me. It showed me how to cause the wall-hangings to ripple as if a wind passed through the chamber, and how to extinguish a candle with but a thought.

Because of this, rumors flew among the servants that our house was bedeviled by hobgoblins and imps. My father sneered at such talk, yet many of our servants left us, and those that stayed would whisper their prayers as they went about the house at night.

Thus, I learned that my gift was not a common skill, but one that was likely to get me burned as a witch if I did not take care. So I practiced alone, following the hushed instruction of the voice in my head.

Yet Lettie stayed. She spent all the hours of the day in my company, but I grieved each evening, when she left our house for her own children.

It is not mere objects that you can draw to you, The Whisper told me one evening. *You can bring people close too, and hold them there.*

One midwinter day, when I was but four years old, Lettie donned her surcoat and kissed me upon the head. As she took her leave of me from the doorway, I decided to test The Whisper's words. I reached for her, not with my hands, but my mind. I reached into her. I gripped her spirit, the living core of her, as tightly as I had clutched at her legs on other nights, bawling for her to tarry.

She froze upon her path. For as long as I held her within my mind, she was still, stuck fast as a bird caught in lime. I tried to pull; to bring her close and make her wrap her arms around me. Yet I was unpracticed and weak. I lost my grip upon her.

Lettie fell to her knees. Her hands flew to the front of her kirtle, to her heart. "Maghew?" Her eyes were as one who has seen a specter, and I was much afeared that I had injured her very soul. She lifted her skirts and ran to the door.

She never returned.

I let a nervous flutter move through my wings at the memory. I gazed upon the new book, the girl reaching out, eyes alight.

"What if she never returns? What if we can't keep her here?"

It will be your choice, The Whisper said. *But for now, there is another who needs you, even more than she. We must go.*

I nodded. The Whisper was right. The Whisper was always right.

So I shook out my feathers, and took to the skies, searching for the next lonely soul to add to my collection.

Chapter Four

Mum opened the front door with hands clad in yellow gloves. I raised the bag I'd got at the chippy on the way home.

"Great, I'm starving," she said and peeled a rubber glove off with a snap.

The house smelled like pine cleaner, the mail was stacked on the side table, and the dirty plates and cups were gone. All the living room needed was a tree, decorated with the cross-eyed reindeer ornaments we'd made as children, and it would feel like our normal Christmas visit. Mum had reclaimed Grandpa's house from the nightmare of the morning.

I suddenly realized she was talking.

"Sorry, what?"

"I was asking for the food." Mum held her hand out. "Are you okay?"

I gave her the bag. "Yeah. I just have this feeling I've forgotten something."

"I know what you mean. I get that all the time. What books did you get?"

"Oh. None, actually."

"Then maybe that's what you forgot." Mum led me down the hall. "Chloe's here. She's been helping."

Chloe sat at the breakfast table. She was a stony-faced girl, with a grumpy expression permanently etched on her face. A mess of short black hair erupted from her head, with a white streak above one eye. It made her look like a badger. Her temperament was about the same too.

She was seventeen and had been homeschooled for years, due to a "bullying incident" in her early teens. Janet was vague on the details, but it was pretty clear Chloe had been kicked out of school for tormenting some poor classmate.

She glanced up for a second as I came in, then went back to glaring at the table. I wanted to tell her that the role of "moody brat" in this family was already taken. But then I realized we were missing our twelve-year-old ray of sunshine.

"Where's Ollie?"

"He went for a walk on the beach," Mum said. "Do you want to share with us, Chloe?"

Chloe gave a grunt Mum seemed to interpret as "yes," because she grabbed three clean plates from the rack. She took the bag, and split the fish and chips between us.

I picked a fat chip and popped it in my mouth. It was still hot and soft in the middle.

"I'm a vegetarian," Chloe said.

"Sorry." Mum used her fork to scoop away the fish and handed Chloe back the plate.

Chloe shoved it away. "It's touched the fish. Been in the same container."

Still, she made no move to leave. She folded her arms over her shirt, and I noticed it had a grave on it, rotting fingers poking out of the soil.

"So, Grandpa fired you," I said, mouth half-full. "Why was that?" I stopped myself from adding, "your charming personality?"

"Silva," Mum said in her warning tone.

Chloe's face cracked into a pained look. "He didn't exactly fire me."

I swallowed my chip and fixed her with my best death stare.

"He forgot to pay me. I asked him for the money he owed, and he accused me of trying to trick him." Chloe looked at her black painted fingernails.

I kept up the glare. Perhaps she'd gotten greedy, decided she could take advantage of him.

"That's why Janet told me he was acting odd," Mum said.

Chloe nodded. "Yeah, because he's dying."

I blinked. Mum paused, a chip halfway to her mouth. There was a shocked silence.

"It's just an infection," Mum said.

"He has Alzheimer's," Chloe replied. "I know what that means. I clean for the nursing home up the road."

Mum put the chip down. "Grandpa will have years before he's that bad. Good years."

"My mum said he might die if he comes home early," Chloe said. "But that's better than losing his mind."

"I'm bringing him home to help him get better. The hospital is bad for him."

Chloe stood up. "Anyway, he's out of Persil. I'll go to Tesco on Monday, but I'll take the rest of his washing home and do it there so it's clean when he gets back."

"They'll have Persil at the shop on the corner," Mum said. "Wouldn't it be easier —"

"I don't go there," Chloe said flatly.

Interesting. Perhaps she'd got banned. Perhaps she was a shoplifter.

"It's forty quid he owes me. Money's in the tin in the cupboard."

"Of course." Mum pulled out the biscuit tin, prising it open. Mum counted out the notes.

"I'll return his clothes tomorrow." Chloe stomped out.

"I guess she got what she came for," I said.

"Silva," that warning tone from Mum again.

"What? She's the worst."

"Chloe ... was a sweet little girl, but she turned in on herself in her teens. I always thought she'd be an artist or a potter."

I snorted. "A potter? Is that even a job anymore?"

"She liked to carve and sculpt. But she took her grandmother's death hard. Started wearing all black and dyed her hair with that awful streak." Mum looked at me, brow crinkled with worry.

"I won't turn out like Chloe," I said.

Mum didn't look convinced, and for a moment I wanted to tell her what I'd learned. There was magic in the world. And if there was magic, there was hope.

Everything would be okay somehow.

It had to be.

I dreamed of the beach, but the sea was made of paper. I stood on the shore with Grandpa, Mum, and Ollie. The paper-waves shattered over the shingle, crinkling into dry, screwed-up foam. They reached up to me, sucking at my feet. I lost my balance, falling into the white of the water. I struggled, but the paper wrapped around me, pulled me away from the shore, from my family. I kicked, trying to keep my head up, but the current was too strong, pages folding around my arms and legs, enveloping me, dragging me under, into the dark beneath the waves.

I woke to a silent house. I crept through it, feeling uncomfortable. I looked in the bedrooms and the living room before I found a note from Mum on the kitchen table.

Morning sleepyheads, it said. *Didn't want to wake you. You both looked so sweet! Gone to get Grandpa. Back in an hour or so.*

Below Mum's note was Ollie's lazy scrawl, barely bothering to be legible.

THE MAGPIE'S LIBRARY ❦ 47

Out. Back before Mum.

How did he manage to make even his handwriting moody?

I checked the clock, wondering whether I had time to get to the library before she came back, but before I could decide, I heard a car pulling up. I hurried outside to meet them.

In the drive, Mum was opening the passenger door. "Here we go, Dad. Let me help."

Grandpa waved away Mum's offered hand. He leaned on the roof for a moment, and then limped toward the front door. He looked so frail. It was hard to recognize the man who took us on hikes to the hushed yew forests of Kingley Vale or along the gusty tops of the South Downs. The man who'd march ahead as Ollie and I begged him to slow down. He'd laugh, and tell us to keep up, be good soldiers. It had been years since we'd gone hiking. How had I not noticed that?

Finally, he reached the door and looked at me.

"Grandpa?"

Even the wind held its breath. Then that giant smile of his spread across his face. He fumbled in his pocket, pulled out a bag of Jelly Babies and winked.

"Go on, Silva. You remember how to eat them, right?"

"Head first."

He nodded. "That's the merciful way."

I felt like I'd reached the shore after a day adrift. I leapt forward and wrapped my arms around him, inhaling his familiar biscuity smell. But it was tainted by hospital anti-septic, and he felt too thin, not his normal, steadying self.

"Oh, Silva, it's so good to be back."

"Careful," Mum said.

I let go of him.

"Silva, could you put the kettle on?" Mum said.

Behind them, Ollie slumped up the driveway. As he caught sight of Grandpa, a smile twitched at the corner of his mouth. "You're back."

"I certainly am. Large as life and twice as handsome." Grandpa leaned against the wall. "Come in, Oliver my boy. We're about to have tea. Perhaps we could have mince pies, too?"

Mum and I glanced at each other. Then I got it. The cold weather. All of us being on Hayling. "It's not Christmas yet," I said.

Grandpa's brow furrowed. "I know that," he snapped. "It doesn't have to be Christmas to have mince pies."

Ollie's eyes flicked back down to his phone. "I don't like mince pies." He shoved past us and thudded upstairs. Mum hurled a theatrical sigh in his direction, but he ignored her.

In the kitchen, I wiped my eyes on my sleeve, opened the Jelly Babies, and shook them out onto a rose-patterned plate. Grandpa recognized me. The antibiotics were working. It wasn't that big a deal to think it was Christmas, really. The cat-flap clattered, making me jump as Tonic, Janet's other cat, came through.

I made the tea, put it on a tray, and carried it to the front room. As I reached the door, I heard the angry hiss of Mum's quiet argument voice.

"You're not a burden, Dad. Don't talk like that."

"Not yet. But I will be." Grandpa sighed. "It's bad enough forcing down all these ridiculous medicines with all those side-effects."

"You'll keep taking those though, right?"

I held my breath.

"I'll take the pills, but when I say it's time, you'll let me go. You'll be okay with that?"

Mum replied quickly. "I never said I'd be okay with that."

"Don't let them take me to hospital again. Promise."

Mum didn't say anything.

I wanted to burst into the room. Wanted to yell at Grandpa. But instead I coughed before I entered. When I pushed open the door, they were smiling, as if they'd been discussing the weather.

"Ah, tea!" Grandpa said. "Perfect."

Fine. I could do normal too. I stuck a grin on my face and placed the tray on the table carefully. I plonked myself on the sofa as Tonic stalked into the room. She ignored Mum, as usual, and I reached for her, but she deftly dodged my grasp, jumped into Grandpa's lap, and settled there, purring.

"Jelly Babies too," Grandpa said. "Wonderful. You remember how to eat them, right?"

"Um … yeah. Head first?"

"That's the merciful way." He smiled, showing no sign that we'd already had this conversation. I grabbed a Jelly Baby and bit its head off, obediently. It felt too rubbery and stuck to the roof of my mouth.

The doorbell rang.

"I'll get it," Mum said in a fake-cheerful sing-song voice.

A few seconds later, she led her cousin into the room. Tonic bounded over. Janet bent down and tickled behind her ears. She was the one who'd chosen the stupid names. She said she liked to go into the garden each night and yell "Gin and Tonic!" She laughed at her stupid joke every time she told it.

Chloe followed her mother, carrying a washing basket full of folded clothes and bedding.

Tonic hissed as Chloe entered, and then ran out into the hall. My smile widened. They do say animals can tell when someone's not right.

"How wonderful to see you home," Janet said. "You seem so much better."

Grandpa sat up. "Being out of that place will do me the world of good. I'll be better in a jiffy. Just need some rest and a couple of cans of … you know. The black stuff. Full of iron."

"Guinness," Mum said.

Janet clasped her hands together. "We just popped in to bring your laundry back."

I wondered how long they'd been waiting for the sound of the car before they "just popped in." There was an awkward pause. Normally, Grandpa would offer a cup of tea or break the tension with a joke. But he just sat there.

"Okay," Janet said. "Chloe will make the bed up."

"That's kind," Mum said. "I'm sure Silva would like to help, too."

I scowled, but Mum gave me one of her looks. I rolled my eyes and followed Chloe as she stomped up the stairs, wondering how such a small person could have so heavy a tread.

I paused as we reached Grandpa's bedroom. I wasn't usually allowed in there. But Chloe shoved the door open without hesitating. It was a plain blue room with a double bed in the center, sheets missing. Chloe thumped the basket down. She wore a black long-sleeved T-shirt with a rotting zombie in lurid reds and greens. It gave me the creeps.

"Doesn't that stuff give you nightmares?" I said, pointing at it.

She peered down at her shirt, then grinned. "I love horror. Dad got me into it. We watch loads when I'm visiting him. And I have nightmares whatever I watch, anyway."

"Mum won't let us watch horror films."

Chloe pulled a sheet from the basket. It crackled with static as she shook it out. "They're the only honest stories.

Romances end with kisses and that, but what about when the couple dies? All stories are horror stories, eventually."

"Wow. That's a cheerful world view."

She started tucking in the sheet at the top of the bed. "If you're just going to stand there, at least hold this." She grabbed something from behind one of the pillows and shoved it at me. I took it automatically. It was only once I felt the cold porcelain in my hands that I looked down.

It was a doll. A doll with golden ringlets, black eyes, and a red dress.

Margaret's doll. Cold shot through me.

"Why are you looking at it like that?" Chloe asked.

"It ... it's pretty, that's all."

"Don't get ideas. I like it. It's creepy. Uncle Chris promised he'll leave it to me."

I clutched the doll tighter. "You're planning for his death already?"

She picked up the duvet and started shoving it into its cover. "It's inevitable, isn't it?"

"They might find a cure. Make a breakthrough."

"You have to face reality. The longer you fight it, the worse it will hurt." She shook out the duvet with a crack and spread it over the bed.

I wanted to tell her about the library. Shove it in her face, show her there was far more to reality, more to life than someone like her could ever imagine.

"I felt the same way about Gran." She put the covers

on the pillows "There are no miracles coming. Hope's a trap." She held out a hand. "Give it here."

I didn't move. She grabbed one of the doll's arms and pulled it from me. She sat it up, against the headboard. "All done." Chloe stomped out.

I stood in the bedroom alone, ears ringing, staring at the doll from Margaret's story.

What was it doing here?

I had to get back to the library. Had to find out.

Chapter Five

Later that morning, Mum made me promise to watch Grandpa while she drove to Bedford to get work stuff and more clothes. I begged for permission to go back to the library, and she said we all had to make sacrifices to help with Grandpa.

But she still let Ollie go for a walk on the beach, which was massively unfair.

I paced the house, frustrated as the time passed. I wasn't needed at all. Grandpa napped. His snores made their way through to my room. Would he even notice if I left? I had to know more about the doll, about Margaret's story, about what it all meant. I wandered downstairs, torn.

The TV blared in the front room, which meant Ollie must be back from the beach. He'd be slumped on the couch, no doubt, playing games on his phone. A voice in my head pointed out that it was his turn to watch Grandpa. After all, he'd been out already, while I'd had to stay in all morning.

"I'm going out for a bit," I shouted at the closed

door. "Grandpa's asleep. Keep an eye on him. I'll be back before Mum."

Ollie didn't reply, which I knew was moody pre-teen for "okay, but I'm not happy about it," so I slipped out into the drizzle before he could change his mind.

I'd nearly reached the library when I heard my name.

"Silva!" The voice was weakened by the wind.

I turned. Approaching from a side street was Chloe, her black coat flapping around her legs, hood up against the driving rain. "Where are you going?"

"The library. Where did you come from?"

She looked annoyed at the question. "Home."

"Home is that way," I pointed the way I'd come.

"I take a different route."

I blinked through the rain. "A longer route? In this weather?"

She shrugged. "Whatever. I'm going to the chemist's to get foot powder for Mum."

"Well, I don't want to hold you up."

Chloe gave a grunt, but she turned away and crossed the road. I watched her until she disappeared into the chemist's, wondering what she was really up to.

By the time I reached the library, I was shivering. I dripped over the floor, and got a sympathetic smile from Asha, at her desk.

"Are you okay? Do you need anything?"

I shook my head. As soon as she turned away, I hurried toward the romances, throat blocked with a lump of mingled hope and worry. What if I found a blank wall?

But the door was exactly as I remembered. I pressed my fingers against the rough old wood, and once again it swung open at my touch.

It was good to be inside. The stone walls and twisting branches made me feel safe, surrounded by stories. I walked around the circle of the library, running my fingers over the shelves as they flowed up the walls like a maze.

The unease had gone, that mental itch like I'd forgotten something. It had been soothed by the comfort of the magical books, as easily as wiping a smear from a mirror.

The magpie perched on the chair in the center. As I approached, the bird lifted its head up to watch me, like a child. I was captivated by the gloss of its wings, its smooth dark head. I reached a hand toward it, then twitched back.

"Can I ... can I stroke you?"

The magpie bounced along the chair arm, toward my hand. I held it out, like I did for Janet's cats, so they could sniff it before I stroked them. But the magpie nuzzled right into my palm. Its feathers were downy, and I could feel the delicate bird skull through them. Warmth grew in my chest for this trusting little creature. I stroked its black-and-white wings and ran a gentle finger down the sharp angle of its tail.

"I can't stay long. I've got to get back before my grandpa wakes."

The bird's tail drooped.

"He has a doll, just like the one in Margaret's story. Why?"

The magpie looked at the shelves. One of the books rustled, edged its way off the branch, and took flight. I reached up as it flapped over my head, and the pages brushed my fingertips before it banked around and swooped toward me. I held my hands out flat, and it landed in my palms. The cover with the girl in the pale nightgown faced me: Margaret's story.

I opened the book toward the end, looking for where the story had left off last time.

Margaret heard crying, in the next room, breathless and weak, from the younger girl who had just arrived here.

I kept turning, glancing at each page, not pausing long enough for the letters to move. I flicked through the scenes: Margaret waited for lights out. Her brother arrived, and then left.

I was almost at the end of the story. Only a few pages left.

Margaret went into the dollhouse. Margaret chose a doll. But when I turned the page, I found it was the last. I traced the words down to the final line.

The doll's hand was warm as it touched Margaret's fingertips. She fell forward, into its merciful embrace.

The story about the creepy dollhouse simply stopped.

"Why does the book end there?" I asked the magpie.

The bird shook its head.

I sighed. "Maybe I'll read another, then."

I went on tiptoes, and slid the book into its place on the shelf. But it was almost out of reach, and as I shuffled forward, stretching up, I tripped on the root. I threw a hand out to break my fall, and in one clumsy motion, knocked a load of books onto the floor.

"Oh, sorry!" I ducked down to gather them up, piling them into my arms.

I put them back on the shelf and reached for the last one, still lying on the dark stone. But as soon as I picked it up, I could feel there was something wrong with it. It was too light, and the stiff covers touched.

I opened it and gasped.

There were no pages. The paper had been ripped out of the spine.

Cold crept up my neck. I stared at the torn scraps of pages, not a fragment of a word visible on any of them. The stumps of pages fluttered under my fingers.

The magpie cawed, a harsh note cutting through the silence. It swooped down, toward my face. I stumbled back. The broken book slipped from my fingers. It hit the floor with a slap. The magpie landed next to it. It ruffled its feathers and stared down at the damaged story.

"What happened to it?"

The magpie put a claw on the front of the book. It looked up at me, eyes glistening. The cover had been torn, the top layer ripped away, leaving only bare cardboard and the very bottom of the picture, which showed a rich red carpet with a chess board on it. There had probably been someone playing chess in the picture, but there was now a gash, a space where the person should have been.

There were no letters in the book to move onto my hands, no pages to be pulled into.

"I can't read that one."

The magpie nodded. It picked the book up with one claw latched onto the spine, and flew back to the shelf it had fallen from, the beat of its wings heavy with the weight of the damaged book. It laid it down, then hopped and flew up the branches, jumping from one to another until it reached a perch near the top, next to a thick paperback.

The story gave a rustling shiver, then it inched itself out, as if pulled by an unseen hand. Like Margaret's, it took flight, swooping around the room, pages opening and closing in the gentle, impossible motion of flight, in spite of its size.

It landed heavily in my hands. On the glossy cover, a girl my age stood in front of a film screen. Her hairstyle was a messy bob, and her clothes looked really dated. She wore a silver dress and reached a hand toward the glowing figure projected in front of her. I could only see a sliver of her face in the semi-darkness of the cinema, but something about the girl caught my attention.

I opened the book and flipped through it. About forty pages in, the story stopped. But it was a magic book, after all. Perhaps it filled itself in as you read it.

I took it to the chair and sat down, shifting on the cushion until I was comfortable. I opened it at the start. Maybe that was my mistake last time, reading too close to the end.

Beth wanted to skip as they walked along the street, but she was too cool for that. She felt cool. Her cousin had done her hair and makeup.

The words wiggled. They detached from the page and scurried toward my fingers.

She'd added a streak of purple next to Beth's face, and styled it to be just messy enough.

I turned over my palm, and a line nestled there, like a moving tattoo.

She'd loaned Beth one of her dresses too. A clingy thing in Beth's favorite color, although Beth worried that she didn't have enough for it to cling against, yet.

The letters kept crawling on to me, a paragraph at a time.

It was almost like they were sisters, or best friends. And for a while, Beth could forget everything that had happened.

Once all the letters had left the page, it rippled, swirling like a white mist. The text tightened.

I took a deep breath, and it pulled me in.

Chapter Six

I was in another body. I was Beth, feeling the swish of a short silver skirt against my bare legs, feeling grown up and a little chilly. A girl giggled next to me. Her ridiculously big hair and blue eyeshadow was like something out of *Flashdance*, which I'd watched once when I was sick and couldn't find the remote. So this book was probably set in the 1980s.

"Stop it, Beth," the girl said. "You're too much."

Beth laughed too, a laugh that brimmed with warmth, with the feeling of being included.

There was a dream-like familiarity to the street, as if I were in a twisted version of a well-loved place. Even the girl next to me reminded me of someone. But the connections stayed out of reach, held at arm's length by Beth's thoughts.

We had all afternoon! Film first, then burgers and milkshakes.

That sounded perfect. I could leave behind the mess of my life and my concerns about Grandpa. I could sink into this story, into Beth's giggles and excitement.

My cousin is so cool. I wish I were that cool.

I let go of my worries and fears. Let go of myself. I relaxed into being Beth.

The wind blew away the stale feeling that had been haunting me. Cars swooshed by, a couple of them beeping at us. I watched my cousin from the corner of my eye, copying her walk: shoulders back, tossing my hair. She could get into clubs, even though she was only sixteen.

I tried not to shiver. I should have worn a coat, but she hadn't, and I wasn't going to hide the dress she'd lent me under the ugly wax jacket Dad had bought. I missed Mum's choice in clothes, missed shopping with her.

No. I wouldn't think about that. I had mascara on. I didn't want it to run.

The cinema marquee came into view: A FISH CALLED WANDA and CHILD'S PLAY spelled out in large black letters.

My footsteps slowed. "You're sure I can pass for fifteen?"

"They won't look twice." My cousin flicked her hair back and held the door.

I put a hand on my hip and sashayed in, trying not to look like a thirteen-year-old. It smelled of stale popcorn. A group of older teens huddled by the ticket desk: two boys and a blond girl.

One of the boys spotted us. "Look who it is!" he said. A sour expression appeared on the face of the blond girl. My cousin let go of the door and pulled her mouth into a strained smile.

"Oh, hi! Um, Beth, this is Emma, her brother Mark, and ... Tom."

Tom. Oh, this was the famous Tom my cousin couldn't stop talking about. She'd said he looked like Patrick Swayze. I squinted. I couldn't see it.

"And who's Beth? Your best friend?" The blond girl said with a nasty grin.

I stuck out my chest, such as it was.

"She's my cousin. I'm ... looking after her."

Looking after? My mouth fell open.

Tom spoke. "I've dragged these two out to see *Child's Play.* How about you?"

My cousin gave me a glance, eyebrows raised as if asking permission. I didn't want to disappoint her, so I gave a hesitant nod. A smile broke over her face.

"That's what I'm here to see!"

My stomach sank. I wanted to see *A Fish Called Wanda*, but I didn't want to sit in the dark cinema on my own. I didn't want to give the memories a chance to creep in.

"Me too," I said in a small voice.

"How old are you?" Emma asked.

"Uh ... fifteen."

She giggled, putting her hand over her mouth. "Well, I'm terribly sorry, but *Child's Play* is an eighteen. Perhaps you two should see the children's film together."

A Fish Called Wanda wasn't a children's film. I let my gaze fall to the tatty carpet of the cinema, dotted with the black ovals of old gum.

"*Child's Play* is a horror, kid," Tom said, softly. "Probably too scary for you."

"You can see *A Fish Called Wanda*. I'll catch you after, okay?" my cousin asked.

What could I say? I'd been daft to think she saw me as a friend. This was a pity trip.

I nodded. She hurried to Tom and they bought tickets. As they walked into the cinema, she gave me a thumbs-up behind Tom's back.

I dragged myself to the ticket office, feeling like a total Billy-no-mates. The man behind the counter was half-hidden behind a magazine with a bikini-clad model on the cover.

"One for *A Fish Called Wanda*." My voice was a petulant whine.

He peered over the magazine. "How old are you?"

"F … fifteen."

"Date of birth?"

I tried to do the math. "March 4, 1972?"

He rubbed at his stubble. "That makes you sixteen."

"Sorry, yeah. I'm sixteen."

He raised the magazine without another word. I stared at it. The cover girl filled out her bikini in a way that made the silver dress feel like a silly costume. I backed away, out through the doors onto the main road, imagining Emma's laughter following me.

"Kid," Tom had called me. I'd been stupid to think I could pass for fifteen. Stupid to think my cousin was a real friend. She'd felt sorry for me, like everyone else. I kicked an empty cola cup at a magpie, wishing the bird was Emma.

It flapped its wings, jumping neatly to one side. Then it sat there, watching me. I felt bad. It wasn't the bird's fault that my life sucked.

"Sorry," I mumbled.

It nodded, tilted its head in a way that seemed sympathetic, and hopped toward the alleyway at the side of the cinema before peering back at me. It nodded, as if encouraging me to come too. I hesitated. But it wasn't like I had anything better to do. I followed the magpie. Just to see where it was going.

I turned the corner and the bird was gone. I took a few steps into the alleyway trying to work out where it had got to. There was no sign of it, but set into the side of the cinema was an old wooden door, with the silhouette of a magpie burned into it. I approached, mouth open. It seemed much older than the wall it was a part of. I poked it. It swung open a few inches to reveal a dim, carpeted space before the door shut.

I pushed it all the way open and stepped inside, out of the wind and the cold.

It was a cinema foyer, but a very different kind from the tatty one I'd just been in; this one was like something out of Hollywood, and bigger than a London multiplex. The carpet was deep, and it silenced my footsteps. There was no ticket office, just six corridors branching out from a central entrance.

The magpie stood to one side, watching.

"Hello?" No one answered.

It was impossible, of course. That thought made me

giddy. An impossible cinema. I giggled, then shut my mouth, embarrassed at how young I sounded.

Down the first corridor, many doors and posters were set into the walls. How many screens did this place have? I drifted along the hallway, as if caught in a dream. The nearest poster showed a boy, creeping through a museum filled with strange objects. There was no title, no tag line, but it looked like a children's film. I tried to ignore the wave of shame, the memory of Emma's face.

I didn't want a kid's film.

The next poster had a girl in an attic, wearing an old-fashioned maid's uniform. She leaned toward a model train set. Historical drama, no doubt. Not my kind of thing.

I wanted a horror film.

I kept going, glancing at the posters: a girl with sores on her face. That might be a medical drama. I couldn't bear anything that would feature a hospital. Not after the horrific hours we'd spent there after we heard about Mum's accident, hoping for a miracle that hadn't come.

The next poster showed a boy running across a dark moor. Definitely horror, from the look on the boy's face. But what was chasing him? Zombies? Vampires? Werewolves?

It didn't matter. I wasn't afraid. I was totally old enough for a horror film. I'd show Emma, I'd show Tom. There was no stupid man at the ticket desk to stop me here.

I pushed open the door and strode in.

My eyes took a few seconds to adjust. Black and white dots danced across the screen to my left. To my right, empty seats rose in rows. There was a rush of color on the screen, and I turned toward it. There were no opening credits, no trailers. The film cut right to a boy: the boy from the poster, hissing blackness flickering behind him.

The screen warped, and the boy leaned out. He held a hand toward me — a hand made of light. Static scurried over his fingers. What was this? An amazing 3D illusion?

I reached toward the boy, expecting my hand to pass through him. But instead, our fingers linked. I gasped and tried to pull back. He held me firmly. The projected light worked its way over his skin and onto mine. It climbed up my arm: a whispering, crackling itch. It spread up to my shoulder, across my chest. I shivered as the dancing static covered my whole body.

The boy's grip tightened. He pulled me into the screen.

I found myself sitting in the wooden chair, back in my own body. The golden motes of the magpie's library floated in front of me, bright as the projected light from Beth's story.

The magpie perched on one of the highest shelves.

"That was amazing." A bow from my host. "But it seemed familiar in places."

The magpie tilted its dark head.

"Like, that girl, on the cinema poster, with sores on her face. She looked exactly like one of Margaret's dolls. Are the stories linked, somehow?"

An enthusiastic nod.

"Like a massive series? Is there another book where Margaret's story continues? Is that where I find out what it has to do with Grandpa?"

I froze as soon as the word escaped my mouth. *Grandpa*.

I pulled out my phone: 3:48 p.m. Grandpa would definitely be awake. Mum would be on her way back from Bedford. I had to beat her home, or I'd have some serious explaining to do.

The magpie flew down to the chair, but I was already backing away.

"I have to run. Sorry. But I'll be back as soon as I can."

It dropped its head, dejected.

I reached out with a finger and stroked the magpie. It pushed up into the motion, as if reveling in my touch.

It was a wrench to leave, painful to step out into the dullness of the everyday. Leaving the beauty of the library felt like losing something vital, like yanking the magic from my soul. The lack was an ache in my bones. My shoulders slumped as the weight of the world settled on me.

Outside, I forced myself to hurry along Elm Grove, fighting the feeling that I should be going back to the library. The same feeling I had before — that I'd forgotten something. Something more important than my phone or my keys. Something I couldn't do without.

The sound of a fire engine cut through my tangled thoughts. The red seemed too bright, the keen of the siren too loud, making my head pound. It sped down the main road, cars pulling over either side. The siren cut out as it turned left, toward Grandpa's cul-de-sac.

I walked faster. Dread ballooned in my gut. Didn't they sometimes send fire engines ahead of an ambulance? No. It had to be going somewhere else. I was being paranoid.

I broke into a jog.

By the time I reached the cul-de-sac, a stitch ached in my side. I turned the corner and my blood froze.

The fire engine sat outside Grandpa's house.

On its high branch, the girl's book was no longer alone. Another volume nestled beside it. She had returned to me. Silva had reached out to me, stroked me with such delicate kindness that I felt the old ache of love well up within me once more.

You do not hide your damaged books well enough, The Whisper said. *You were never good at hiding things.*

"I wish she could stay here, as she was today; not sealed within the pages of her book."

You know none will choose to stay with you. You have to take them. Do not get attached to her. You have been hurt enough in the past.

That had been the hard lesson of my life.

After Lettie left, Father sent for a tutor, claiming a man would be less given to witless superstition. Thus, I was placed with a teacher who beat my lessons into me. I was being punished for what I had done to Lettie, although none would acknowledge it. I wondered if they knew of the power I had, and what I had done to her soul.

I rarely saw my father. Perhaps he would not have minded that I was unable to ride if I knew Latin or Greek. Perhaps he would not have called me a slugabed if I could shoot a bow and arrow. But my sicknesses often kept me from both my tutor and my duties.

Yet I was not alone. I had the silky voice of The Whisper, and my siblings began to slip into my chamber to see me. First was my sister Isabel. She remembered when I was but a babe, and had heard rumors from the servants that said I was owl-blasted or devil-touched. But she found no such demon child, only a small boy in a dark room. So she tarried to talk with me.

After that, my brothers, James and Edmund, and my sisters, Elizabeth, Alice, and Eleanor came to greet me too. I became their pet. I was hungry for their stories, for their tales of the world, and they were happy to find an audience that attended upon their every word.

I was not permitted to go outside. The doctors said the corrupt London airs would hurt me, that the stinking mists of the sewers and rivers could infect my blood. Thus, to my young mind, the city air was not just unhealthful; it was poisonous, and I listened to my siblings play in the knot garden with the fear their laughter would at any moment turn to choking. Their visits were the only light in my little life, and I wished they would remain close to me, and safe.

Yet, one by one, I lost them. Father sent James up north to manage our estates after many tenants were lost to the sweating sickness, a terrible disease where a man could be well in the morning, have the sweat take him at noon, and be dead before dinner. Edmund went to Oxford, then to practice law in London. Elizabeth was married and moved to her new husband's home.

For a while, I still had my other sisters. Eleanor and Alice visited me together, sitting on either side of my pillow. They brought me the gossip from the city and the news from court. Isabel brought me sweets taken from the table: marzipan and gingerbread. She brought me the scent of her rosewater and the herbs she wore in her pomander.

But the seasons continued to turn, and the years with them, pushing us apart like the spinning of a wheel. I was losing my sisters to the delights of the city, to Whitsunday fairs and May Day mummers, masques and markets bright with ribbons and fine fabrics. The distances of the world grew between us. Within another year, Eleanor and Alice were married, and left us.

Only Isabel, my dear Isabel, still had time for me. She sat close, drawing pictures with her hands as she shared stories, true and invented, about the seven of us, tales that always ended in Happily Ever After.

Yet Father made Isabel spend much of her time learning prayers, working on her embroidery and her music, so she would be ready for marriage. Thus I was alone for many dark hours. I began to use my gift to borrow trinkets from my siblings, to slip them away unseen. I thought of my keepsakes as holy relics, like saints' bones or the rosary of a martyr.

It was The Whisper's idea. It understood the loneliness in my core, and bade me to take things to ease it. The small treasures I spirited away did help: a bracelet from Elizabeth; the brooch James used to pin feathers upon his cap; Edmund's intaglio ring. I wished to take Isabel's silver pomander and hold the scent of her lavender and rosemary, but there would be no hiding the sweet air it gave. I borrowed her doll instead, and would act out my own stories, pretending Isabel was there with me.

I had no golden reliquary in which to store my treasures, like the relics at the cathedral, so I tucked them within my blankets, surrounding myself with reminders of the family I loved. Perhaps my relics could work miracles too. Perhaps they could bring us back together.

However, as The Whisper said, I did not hide them well enough.

"Why does it matter if Silva sees my damaged books?"

None can know how your stories were taken from you. They may try to steal more.

"But Silva ..."

The girl's book has a companion. You should be filling it, instead of tarrying here, arguing with me. Come, let us fly.

Reluctantly, I nodded, and set about my work once more.

Chapter Seven

I sprinted along the pavement, past the fire engine, breath coming in desperate gasps. I slipped on the shingle of Grandpa's driveway and landed on my knees. Pain jarred through me. I dragged myself to my feet and dashed for the house, ignoring the hot throb of my hands where I'd grazed them.

The hall reeked of smoke. Not the comforting smoke of a bonfire, but the chemical stench of burning plastic. In the kitchen, the air was smoggy, but there were no flames.

A firefighter sat at the table, helmet on his lap. Beside him, Grandpa held his head in his hands. He looked up when I came in, worry in his eyes.

"What happened? Is Ollie okay?" I pressed a hand against the stitch in my side.

"Um ..." Grandpa looked around, as if my brother might be hiding in a kitchen cupboard.

"No one was hurt," the firefighter said, turning awkwardly in his bulky outfit. "Just a little accident." He waved a hand toward the stove.

On the burner stood the melted remains of something

THE MAGPIE'S LIBRARY 75

plastic. White foam coated it like snow, and a scorch mark flowed up the wall.

"I'm so sorry," Grandpa said.

"No need to apologize, although you should see a doctor. Smoke inhalation can be serious."

His voice trembled. "I got mixed up. Put the new kettle on the hob. Forgot you plug this one in. Such a silly mistake."

Beige plastic showed in the un-charred sections of the melted lump. An electrical cord snaked out the back, almost burned through. It wasn't a new kettle. He'd had it for years.

My pulse pounded through my ears.

"It's lucky your neighbor heard the alarm. No serious damage here."

Neighbor? Janet was involved?

The firefighter stood. "Don't use the oven until you've had it checked out properly."

"I would offer you a cup of tea." Grandpa closed his eyes. "I'm such a silly old fool."

The firefighter shook his head. "Don't be so hard on yourself." But he leaned toward me on his way out and lowered his voice. "Perhaps you could keep an eye on him."

I nodded at his retreating back, feeling sick. Mom would be furious. I was meant to be keeping an eye on him, but I'd asked Ollie. Where was he?

The toilet flushed upstairs. That answered that.

He'd probably had his headphones on, blasting one of his stupid games too loud to hear a smoke alarm. The thudding of footsteps came down the staircase. I turned to the door, ready to shout at him.

But it wasn't Ollie. It was Chloe.

"You were at the library for a long time," she said as she walked into the kitchen.

Grandpa ran a hand through his thin hair. "I'm so sorry."

The windows were open, the chill of outside creeping into the kitchen. But the acid of the smoke burned at the back of my throat.

"It's lucky Chloe heard the alarm. I didn't think to use the extinguisher like she did. I just ... panicked."

Chloe shrugged. "I panicked too. Didn't need to call 999."

"You did the right thing," Grandpa said.

I stared at the mess on the stove. I had to sort it before Mum came home. I didn't know how to get the melted plastic off, and it needed to cool first anyway. A soot stain stretched over the sunflower tiles, a black flame. I grabbed the sponge from the sink, and started wiping at the burn mark. It smeared over the wall.

"Don't do that, Silva," Grandpa said. "I'll clean it up. You girls should sit down."

I kept scrubbing. "You're meant to be resting, and I don't mind."

"I do." Grandpa's tone was firm. "Get out of this smoke. I'll join you in the front room with some Hobnobs."

Chloe slouched out. I put down the sponge, but hovered by the stove.

"Please, Silva. I need a moment alone."

As I drifted along the hall, I caught sight of myself in the gold-framed mirror. My face was white. I pinched my cheek, but my skin stayed as pale as paper.

Chloe threw herself on the couch, kicked off her shoes, and put her feet up.

"Have you seen Ollie?" I asked.

She shook her head.

I slumped onto the armchair, lowered my head into my hands, and breathed into the darkness of my fingers.

The click of the front door: Mum.

I jumped up, ready to explain, but blue Converse trainers flew across the hall as Ollie kicked them off. My emotions hardened into anger.

"What's that smell?" Ollie peered into the front room. The smoggy air made him look fuzzy at the edges, and my exhaustion added a tinny buzz to his voice.

"Uncle Chris almost burned down the house," Chloe said.

I snapped around. "That's not ..." I turned back to Ollie. "I asked you to stay here and watch him."

"No, you didn't."

I put my hands on my hips. "Yes, I did."

"In fact, I heard Mum ask you to watch him. Right when I left."

I froze. That wasn't right.

Oh no. Oh no.

I didn't actually see Ollie. I shouted through the door. I'd assumed he was in the front room. But what if he'd just left the TV on, or Grandpa had?

"But … you've been gone forever, then!"

He shrugged. "The fire got put out, right?"

Chloe nodded.

"Then I'm going up to bed. I'm tired." Ollie stomped up the stairs.

I dropped into the armchair, picked up a cushion, and hugged it. This was all my fault. I'd left Grandpa alone. What was I going to tell Mum?

Chloe interrupted my thoughts. "What d'you think Uncle Chris is going to do now?"

"What do you mean, 'do now'?"

"Well, he doesn't want to go in a home, and he knows he can't live alone."

"Why not?"

"Might burn the place down."

Her words were like a punch. "No. He has to fight this."

"Why?"

I clenched my jaw. "Because we love him and want him to live."

"What about what he wants?"

I clutched the cushion tighter. The fabric bunched up under my fingers.

"My gran fought it to the bitter end, you know. Had all the treatments, even when they made her worse." Chloe stared out of the window as she talked, as if it meant nothing to her, her face set in its usual marble frown. "Death is inevitable."

"But ... he ..."

Chloe stiffened. "I should go."

"Hang on ..."

But she stomped to the front door and let herself out. A second later, she ran past the window, across the front lawn, waving her arms, mouth moving as she shouted something I couldn't catch through the double-glazing. I hurried over to see what she was doing, but she was already out of sight.

A red car turned onto the cul-de-sac. Mum.

I rushed to the hall, throat dry, trying to work out what I was going to say, but the bang of the car door came too quickly, followed by the sound of keys in the lock.

"I'm back!" Mum hunched over from the weight of the bags slung over her shoulders. She dropped everything in the hall with a grunt, and her nose wrinkled. "What's that smell?"

"Um, there was a little accident."

Footsteps thudded down the stairs. "Did you bring my Xbox?"

"Nice to see you too, Ollie. It's in one of the bags. What kind of accident?"

"Grandpa's fine. It's just the kettle," I said quickly.

Ollie dropped to his knees and inspected the bags. "Chloe said he almost burned the house down."

It would be so easy to kick him, from where I stood.

Mum's eyes widened. "What? Where is he?"

"In the kitchen," I said. "Chloe was exaggerating."

Mum peered down the hall. Then she waved her hands to shoo us into the front room together. She shut the door and lowered her voice. "Almost burned the house down?"

Ollie pulled his Xbox from a bag and crawled with it under one arm over to the TV.

"Grandpa put the plastic kettle on the stove," I said. "Got it mixed up with his old metal one. It melted, but everything's fine. No big deal."

"He got confused?"

"It's the infection, right? He'll be okay."

Ollie peered at the back of the TV. "Mum, did you bring the HDMI cable?"

"The what?"

"To connect it. Won't work without it."

Mum put her fingers on her temples and rubbed. "I don't think so."

Ollie sat back on his heels. "Then what was the point of bringing the Xbox at all?"

Mum spun around. "I have more important things to

worry about than your bloody video games right now, Oliver." She turned back to me. "Sorry, Silva. You were explaining."

I didn't want that anger directed at me. "That's ... it. The fire engine came, but it was sorted by then."

"Ollie was talking about Chloe. What was she doing here?"

I licked my lips. "She ... called 999. Put the fire out with the extinguisher."

Mum stood perfectly still. When she spoke, it was very slowly.

"Why didn't you do that?"

The words were as dry as paper in my throat. "I was at the library."

"Silva," her voice had a hard edge. "I told you to stay here with your grandfather."

"I thought Ollie was watching him."

"I asked you, not Oliver."

"Silva didn't ask me," Ollie said.

I could have slapped him. I seriously could have. "I thought I did, but he was gone all day. He only just got back."

Mum swiveled around to my brother. "Oliver?"

"I needed some air."

"I'm going to have words with both of you." Mum's eyes glistened. She wiped a hand across them. "But I have to speak to your grandfather. I expect he's upset right now."

I nodded, trying to ignore the lump in my throat.

"Go to your rooms. Now."

I woke hours later. It was dark, but the mutter of TV came from downstairs. I felt odd, craving something I couldn't put my finger on. Something was missing. I got out of bed and tiptoed into the hallway, wondering if I was hungry. But that didn't feel right.

I peered into Mum's room. She twitched in her sleep, brow furrowed. She was prone to nightmares, but this one didn't seem bad and I wasn't ready to face her, so I left her sleeping and crept down the stairs.

Grandpa sat in the front room, a Guinness in his hand, and a paper with a half-filled crossword in his lap. He jumped when he saw me in the doorway. Put a hand on his chest. "You almost gave me a heart attack."

I climbed onto the couch and wrapped my arms around his chest, my face against his shirt. I breathed in the smell of him: musty aftershave and digestive biscuits.

"I love you," I said.

"I love you too." He patted my back. His soft stomach moved with his breath. Out, in.

"I missed you." I sat up. "I wish we lived down here. Or in one place, at least."

"That's my fault. I dragged your gran and your mother all around the country in my army days. Got her used to moving." He pressed his lips together. "You look pale. Are you okay?"

I wracked my brain for something to say. Something that would make this feel normal. "How's the puzzle going?" A few clues were completed in Grandpa's neat handwriting.

"It's tough. And that's the problem." His hazel eyes were intense under his bushy brows. "My brain feels like an old jigsaw. Pieces are starting to go missing."

"You were okay this summer."

"I was hiding it, best I could. But it seems I can't hide it anymore."

A cold kind of seasickness sloshed through my stomach. "There ... there are breakthroughs all the time. Maybe there'll be one for Alzheimer's."

"There won't be a cure for old age. It's not just the Alzheimer's, it's my heart, and my back and knees. It's painful to move, and you know how I loved walking." Grandpa put his can down. "When I'm gone, promise me you'll stride over the South Downs, with the wind in your face and the clouds scuttling above. Think of me walking up there with you, and be happy."

My vision blurred. "Don't say that!"

He reached for my hand. "I'm sorry I didn't remember you in that hospital. That's not right, and I don't want you to think it's because you aren't important to me. My family is all I have. I never want to forget you again."

All the words I wanted to say clotted in my throat. I wanted to tell him that he was my anchor in the ever-shifting sea of my life. I wanted to tell him I loved him fiercely, and he had to get well. My cheeks were wet. My nose was running. I needed to wipe my face on my sleeve, but he clutched my fingers tightly.

"Grandpa, I ..." There was a hot knot in my chest. I tried to exhale, but my breath caught on it, and a sob came out, swallowing my words. I buried my head in his shoulder

"I know it's hard to say goodbye. I've had to do it too many times." I listened to his breath, his pulse, felt his warmth. "It feels like yesterday when my little sister, Janet's mother, died. Your grandmother was in her thirties. My other sister died in a sanatorium at about your age. But I'm an old man. I've had a good life."

A word cut through the panic, cut through the tears, and snagged on my attention. I pulled back. "A sanatorium?"

"Yes. It was where they sent people who had tuberculosis, before we got antibiotics."

Cold crawled up my spine. "Wait. What was her name?"

"My older sister? Margaret."

The room spun. "Margaret?"

Grandpa rolled up his sleeve, revealing his tattoo. "She loved dolls. I got this as soon as I was old enough. So she'd always be with me."

Chapter Eight

I tried to stop my thoughts whirling. Tried to breathe normally.

Margaret was a real person, not just a character in a book. Margaret was my great-aunt.

Grandpa picked up his can, slurped at his Guinness.

"It's Margaret's doll in your room? She died?"

"That's her photo over there." He nodded at the shelves. "It's funny how much easier it is to remember things from back then. It's clearer than last year."

I stood, and looked at the picture. I'd seen it before, but not paid attention. It was fuzzy, and I'd always found it hard to tell people in old photos apart. There were two children: a girl and a boy. Behind them stood their mother, holding a baby. Now I stared closely, I could tell the boy was the one who had come to visit Margaret.

The blood pumping in my ears grew louder. Grandpa was Margaret's little brother.

"You went to visit her," I said. "Snuck out, without telling your parents?"

"Yes, the night she died. They found her on the floor in the morning. How did you ..." He rubbed at his forehead with his free hand. "Oh. I've already told you this story. Silly old fool."

"No, I …" I didn't know how to finish the sentence. Didn't know how to say I'd seen him as a little boy through his sister's eyes.

"I'm sorry," he said. "I'm repeating myself."

"No, Grandpa." I climbed back on the sofa, reached for him and squeezed his fingers, staring at the tattoo on his arm, turned green with age. Staring at the ringlets, the black eyes, the once-perfect face of the doll, Margaret's doll, sunken into the old muscle.

Grandpa was saying something.

I shook my head. "What?"

"I said, I shouldn't be putting this on you. I'm getting morose. It's this stuff." He held up his beer. "I need to talk to Janet and your mother. And I need to go to bed."

"Yeah," I said, distracted.

"And so do you, Silva. Come on. I'll turn things off down here. Up you go."

I stumbled into bed still trying to process everything.

Margaret was my great-aunt. She had been an actual living, breathing person. She died without finding the cure she was searching for in the dollhouse.

I tried to focus, but my head buzzed with the static of exhaustion. I listened to the sea until the hiss of the waves sounded like the rustling of pages. Then the bed, the room, Grandpa's home felt insubstantial, as if a gust would blow them all away and reveal the library.

I had to get back there as soon as I could. Had to figure out what this all meant.

I woke to voices arguing downstairs. Janet's nasal tone merged with Grandpa's low rumble and Mum's clipped delivery. My Ravenclaw clock said 8:02 a.m., but the sky was so overcast it could still be night.

I crept down the stairs and peered around the banister.

They were in the kitchen, with the door open. Janet wore her holiday camp uniform: a bright blue receptionist blazer with her name tag on it. Mum was still in her pajamas.

"You can't let him do this," Janet said.

I ducked back before they could see me, and sat on the bottom stair, hidden behind Janet's coat, tossed over the banister. An ache echoed through me, making it hard to concentrate.

"I'm right here, Janet," Grandpa said. "Don't talk about me as if I'm not."

"Someone needs to talk sense into you. I'm here a lot more than she is, and we'll end up dealing with it all when she sods off again."

Mum spoke. "I'm not 'sodding off,' it's just that my job means —"

"Your job means more to you than your family. Moving all over the country, dragging those poor children around, unwilling to commit to anywhere, or anything. Not even their dad."

"Janet!" Grandpa's voice.

I picked at the carpet, working a loop loose. Dad and Mum split when I was little. We visited for a while, but he remarried and had another family. We hardly ever saw him, now.

"You two used to be close," Grandpa said. "What happened?"

"She's the queen of petty grudge-holding," Janet said. "Been angry at me for decades."

"Oh, for goodness sake. I'm not angry at you."

"You're never here. You weren't here when my husband left, or when Mum died, or through Chloe's difficulties. And you won't be here now."

The loop I was fiddling with pulled out of the carpet, leaving a hole in the floral pattern.

"I'm not saying you should go into hospital, Dad …"

"He should." Janet interrupted.

"But there's no reason not to take your medicine."

"Look at them! Just look at them!" I heard Grandpa's footsteps, and then something slammed and rattled: his pill boxes. They usually sat on the counter: translucent red boxes joined in a line, marked with the days of the week, each segment brim-full of pills.

"I can't stand the side-effects. They make me so sick and tired."

"You need them." Janet's voice. "They keep you alive."

"But for what?"

"For us?" Janet said.

"I can't be left alone. Yesterday made that clear. I'm not going into a home, and I'm not having a nurse. It's time for nature to take its course."

I felt as if I were underwater; ears ringing, breath stopped. I put my hand over my mouth and my elbow nudged Janet's coat. Just a tap, but enough to tip it. It hissed as it slid from the banister and hit the ground with a soft thump.

"Is that one of the children?" Janet asked.

A chair scraped across the floor. I tried to stuff the loop of carpet back, gave up, and scurried upstairs. The steps creaked as Mum followed. I made it under the duvet, but her voice came from the doorway.

"Silva, I know you're awake. What did you hear?"

I stared at the green wall in front of me. "Grandpa's not going to take his medicine." I tried to keep my voice steady. "It's my fault, isn't it?"

Her footsteps crossed the floor. "No. Why would you say that?"

"Because I didn't watch him, and now he doesn't trust himself."

The mattress sagged as Mum sat on my bed, tipping me toward her. She laid a hand on my side. "Silva, don't blame yourself, please."

"He'll die without his medicine, right?"

"Not right away."

"Don't let him do this."

It was hard to get the words out. They felt wrong. I shouldn't have to say any of it.

She stroked my hair. "I can't force pills down his throat."

I rolled onto my back and looked up at her. There were dark circles under her eyes, and her short hair was flat, not styled like usual.

"Stay here. We could live here. Then he wouldn't need a nurse."

"But my job ..."

"You don't even like your job. Get another job. One where we can stay in one place."

She pushed my hair behind my ears. "We need the money."

This was an old argument. But today I felt the heat rising, the blood rushing to my head. I batted her hand away.

"I wish things were different, Silva."

I closed my eyes. Pushed hard against the sockets with the heels of my hands. The kettle was my fault. He'd still be taking his medicine if I hadn't left him alone.

"Grandpa is lot better. He has an appointment with the doctor tomorrow morning. If he's on the mend, he'll probably be fine for months. We can head to Bedford in the afternoon, and come back for Christmas, like normal."

I dropped my hands. "We can't leave tomorrow."

"You have school, and I have work." She exhaled. "I shouldn't have been so hard on you yesterday. I'm sorry."

She's letting this happen, a voice in my head said. Janet's right. She cares more about her job than she cares about her family.

"Just go."

"Silva …"

"I said go! Get out of my room!"

"Okay." Mum raised her hands, a shield in front of her. "I love you, Silva."

I stared at the plaster swirls on the ceiling, like albino rainbows, and didn't respond, even when I heard her muffled sob from the hall.

It was Sunday, so the library was closed. I wanted to spend time with Grandpa before we left, so I finally dragged myself down. He seemed more distracted as the morning wore on, not quite following along with the conversation. For lunch, Mum made old-school tacos, a favorite of mine, probably meant as an apology, but I avoided looking at her as I ate. Ollie loaded his up with meat and cheese, avoiding all the vegetables. I made a healthier one, but the hard shell cracked when I bit it, and stabbed into the roof of my mouth. I spat it out.

"Silva," Mum said. I ignored her.

Grandpa paused between bites. "Since it's raining, why not take the children to the cinema?"

"It shut down years ago," Mum said. "It's flats now."

The lost look I'd seen at the hospital reappeared on Grandpa's face for a moment before he pulled his features back into a smile. I pushed away the rest of my taco.

After lunch, Ollie went upstairs while Mum moved Grandpa into the front room and asked me to make tea. I tried not to look at the deflated kettle. Grandpa wouldn't let anyone else clean it up, but he hadn't tried to do it himself.

The steps of making tea felt like random motions, separated from meaning: grabbing the mugs, pouring water, putting them in the microwave. It was all pointless.

That's when they caught my eye: Grandpa's pills.

They sat in their transparent red boxes: his antibiotics, his heart pills, and the others.

Hope jumped in my chest. Mum said she couldn't force medicine down Grandpa's throat, but perhaps we could, in a way. I could slip a couple of Grandpa's pills into his tea. If I made the tea today and tomorrow morning, it might be enough to get him over his infection, at least.

He'd never have to know.

I wandered into the hall to check no one was around. The murmur of conversation came from the front room; Mum and Grandpa.

All clear.

I ducked back into the kitchen, flicked opened the box marked Sunday, and picked a few pills at random. The microwave beeped, and I nearly jumped out of my skin.

Deep breaths. I poured the hot water into the cups. If I just stirred the pills in, they wouldn't dissolve fully. I had to crush them.

Rain pattered urgently against the window, as if hurrying me. I opened cupboards, looking for Grandpa's mortar and pestle, the one he used to grind herbs from his garden. I found it shoved behind some dishes. I glanced outside. The herb beds were overgrown, Ollie's football half-swallowed by them. How long had it been since Grandpa made his own pesto?

A magpie sat on the fence. I gasped. It was the same one, it had to be. I waved.

A flutter and swoop, and it landed on the windowsill. I put my hand against the glass, streaked with raindrops. The magpie hopped closer to my fingers, as if it wanted to feel my touch, even through the window that separated us.

"I wish I could come today, but the library's closed."

In the front room, Grandpa started coughing, bringing my attention back to my task.

"I'll come tomorrow. When they go to the doctors. I promise."

I threw the pills into the stone bowl and ground them until there was nothing but powder. I tipped it into Grandpa's mug. That's when I heard footsteps.

The magpie flew away. I turned, stomach dropping.

Grandpa stood in the doorway. His gaze fell on the

open pill box, on the powdery mortar I held above his mug. "Silva?"

I tried to think of something to say, something to explain away the scene. Pressure built in my head.

Grandpa raised his voice. "Liz! Come here."

Mum hurried in. "Silva! What are you doing?"

The two of them stared, anger in my mother's eyes, disappointment in my grandfather's. The moment stretched out. Blood pounded in my ears.

I dropped the mortar. It hit the counter with a loud crack as I dashed out of the kitchen, past Mum and Grandpa. I grabbed my coat, threw open the front door, and ran into the rain.

"Silva!" Mum shouted.

I didn't look back.

The drizzle stung my eyes and I barely noticed the world, the cars, and the wind that came up from the beach and pushed me along the road. I ran as far as I could stand, until my breath came so hard I doubled over, coughing. No one was shouting my name now. I checked over my shoulder. No Mum. Just a dark figure, a little way behind, hood too low to see their face.

Where could I go, in the rain, on a Sunday? I couldn't stay outside. The pavement was slippery with moss and wet leaves. The tang of sea air was strong, and gulls cried out in the sky above me.

Then another bird joined them. One with dark wings with a flash of white.

My heart soared. My magpie. I reached toward it as it flew overhead. It cawed, the sound almost lost on the wind. I pulled my coat tighter and hurried on. You couldn't expect a magpie to understand Sunday closing. Still, following it was a better option than going home.

A message buzzed through on my phone. I pulled it out: Mum.

Where are you?

If I didn't reply, she'd end up calling the police.

Going for a walk. Don't come after me. I need some time alone.

Dots on my screen as Mum wrote back. They disappeared, as if she'd reconsidered what she was writing and deleted her message. A pause, more dots, and the bubble appeared.

Fine. I could almost hear her sigh. *We'll have a proper talk when you get back.*

As I hurried up the road, I tried to forget the look in Grandpa's eyes. Like I'd betrayed him. I felt a prickle on the back of my neck and glanced over my shoulder.

The dark figure was still there. I'd been walking fast, but they'd kept up. They were probably just hurrying to get home, get out of the drizzle.

Still, I sped up.

The magpie landed on the wall outside the library and waited.

"See," I said, a little out of breath. "It's closed."

The magpie took off again. But it didn't head for the

entrance. It flew around the corner. I followed, across the waterlogged grass that ran down the side of the library, separated from the grounds of the primary school by a chain-link fence.

And there, set into the gray-brick outside wall was the magpie's door.

Excitement rushed through me. Of course the door could be here. It was magic, after all. The door could be anywhere.

"Thank you!" I said out loud, although the magpie had disappeared. It would be waiting inside, no doubt. I ducked out of the rain and into the golden light of the magical library. I shook my damp jacket off, already feeling better.

Outside, the wind had cut through me, the drizzle chilling me. I'd felt fragile, like soggy paper that could fall apart at a touch. Here I felt myself. Felt complete, healed by the magic all around. I took deep breaths, inhaling the invigorating glow of the library.

The magpie sat on the chair.

"I should have realized you wouldn't worry about opening times."

I walked to my feathered friend, and held my hand out. It jumped onto my thumb, and perched there, little claws digging in, but not enough to hurt. Its tail twitched, counterbalancing its weight. I ran a finger over its smooth dark feathers, down its back, to the end of its tail.

"Margaret was my great-aunt," I said.

The magpie nodded, gaze fixed on me.

"Are all these stories about real people?"

Another nod.

"Are they all dead?"

The magpie shook its little head. I exhaled, and the library seemed lighter. I didn't want to think about death right now. But maybe that was the point. Maybe I was meant to remember people, now Grandpa was forgetting. Still, the stories I'd been reading had been a bit depressing.

"Can I have a book where the main character isn't dead?"

The magpie took off from my finger. The removal of its small weight felt like a loss. It flew to one of the branches, near the top. With a whisper of paper, a book eased itself from the shelf and swooped down to my waiting hands.

A familiar girl looked out from the picture on the cover. I almost dropped the book.

"Chloe."

The magpie nodded.

But it wasn't the Chloe I knew now. It was the Chloe I barely remembered: the Chloe who smiled a lot more before she lost her grandmother, before she got into horror, before she got kicked out of school for bullying.

On the cover, she was about my age, long brown hair pulled into a high ponytail. She wore a yellow jumper and stood in a garden filled with statues, reaching out toward the nearest one with an excited expression.

I flipped through to a random page.

Chloe woke on the soft ground.

I carried the book to the chair and sat down.

Time was running out, and she was no closer to finding a solution.

The letters moved, scuttling toward my hands. It felt weird to read this, almost rude. These were Chloe's thoughts.

The park was there for a reason. It had to be.

But I was curious, so I let the words creep over my skin, forming skittering sentences.

You could enter another life. So maybe you could recover from a terminal illness, too.

The words tightened, tying me to the now-blank page.

It stood to reason. Didn't it?

The text pulled me down into the white of the book.

Chapter Nine

I lay on grass: mossy, soft, and comfortable. Vivid green surrounded me, punctuated by the white marble of statue bases. The sun hung close to the horizon and, in the distance, dark walls encircled the park.

I pushed myself onto my knees, and the blood rushed to my head. With it came the memories of another life, the thoughts of another person. Chloe's thoughts.

If only I could hang out here a bit longer.

Her fear was as hard as a stone in my gut: fear for her grandmother. This had to be about four or five years ago, when she was still alive.

But I've been out way too long. I've got to get back. Got to make sure she's okay.

It was hard to keep her thoughts at bay. And I didn't want to. I'd come to the library to forget Grandpa's decision. To forget about the pills and the disappointment on his face. Chloe was worried, but hopeful. She didn't have my guilt, my shame turning her stomach.

So I let myself fall into her feelings. Let them become my own.

I hurried out the magpie's door and the pain of the real world hit. Leaving the park had always been hard, but it was getting way worse. My arms were so heavy my shoulders ached.

The weather didn't help. In the statue garden, a few clouds drifted in the blue sky, pretty and fluffy. But out here they were the gray of old concrete, pushing down on me.

I leaned on the statue in the real park to catch my breath. Lichen spread over the plinth like a nasty scab, unlike the clean white of the statues in the magpie's park.

I had to get home to Gran. She got sad if I was out for more than a couple of hours.

She'd made me promise I'd be there when she died. Made me hold her hand and swear it. I had, but I'd made another promise, after she fell asleep.

I'd promised I'd fix this.

There had to be a solution through the magpie's door. Or what was it for? It had appeared just as Gran got majorly sick. But I'd been into a statue three times now and found nothing. I had to be doing something wrong. Being stupid, as usual.

I'd look closer next time. Think harder.

I wanted to jog home, but my feet were heavy and they dragged. I tripped on the cracks in the pavement. The wind pushed against me, taking my breath, making me feel like crap.

I unlocked the door quietly so I wouldn't let Mum know I'd popped out. I was easing it closed when I spotted her and Uncle Chris in the living room, side by side on Mum's precious new blue sofa. They stared at the carpet, as if they were statues themselves. I froze.

If both of them were here, no one was with Gran. They'd left her alone.

But we never left her alone. We'd been with her every second since she'd got bad. Swapping out to go to the loo, or get a drink. There was only one reason they'd have left her alone.

The world tilted. The front door slipped from my hand and slammed shut. Mum looked up, makeup smeared over her blotchy face. "Chloe, come here. Sit down."

I backed away.

"Chloe." Mum's voice was too kind. Not demanding to know where I'd been, none of the usual grief I got from her. Uncle Chris stared at me with the same red-eyed sympathy.

I ran to the stairs. I had to get to Gran's room without hearing. If I could get up there without Mum saying the words, it'd be okay. I kind of knew that was daft. But it didn't stop me.

"Chloe!" Mum called.

I took the steps two at a time, hand skimming along the banister.

"Chloe! Wait! Don't go in there!"

Gran's room was first on the left. I shut the door behind me. I threw myself into the chair at the side of the bed, taking a deep breath of her lavender perfume.

"Gran, it's me. I'm back." I grabbed her hand. It was limp, but warm. She was sleeping. That's all. She had to be sleeping. I felt for a pulse. Nope. But that didn't mean anything. I'd always been bad at taking my own pulse. I was just having trouble finding Gran's.

"Gran, wake up. Please."

Gran's mouth was slightly open. I willed her chest to move. I held my own breath, listening for the slightest sound from her.

She couldn't be dead. She'd always been there, solid as a statue. We'd lived with her since Dad left. I waited. I wouldn't breathe until she did.

My head spun. The pressure built. Things started to get dark. The stairs creaked as Mum climbed. I couldn't hold it anymore. The air escaped in a rush of breath.

Mum opened the door.

I turned around. "I ... she ..."

Mum put her hand on my shoulder. "I'm so sorry, Chloe."

I swallowed. This wasn't real. Couldn't be. It didn't feel real.

"I said I'd be here. Did she ... ask for me?"

Mum's voice shook. "No, love. She didn't even wake up."

Uncle Chris made tea. He handed me a cup. It was so hot it burned my palms. I clutched it tight, hoping the pain would block out Mum's words, as she told me the details.

Gran died not long after I'd gone out. The doctor had been already. I squeezed the mug tighter, but it was already cooling, the burn of my hands fading as the ache in my chest grew. I put the cup down without drinking any.

Mum and Uncle Chris talked about the funeral: songs Gran would like. Tonic scampered through the door on her too-big kitten feet. I reached for her, but she hissed and swiped a claw. Blood swelled into the thin red lines she'd left. It stung more than it should.

Mum asked if I had ideas for the funeral. But I didn't want to think about Gran's funeral. I didn't want there to be a funeral. I couldn't face it. I muttered about needing some air, and hurried out of the house, to the only place I wanted to go.

In the park, the magpie's door was still there, waiting. I'd thought it might disappear with Gran's life. The life it was meant to save. But it was still here. So I was wrong about that.

I was wrong about all of it.

I didn't go through. I collapsed on the bench and stared at the statue in the center of the small park. She was some distant relative according to Mum, called Cordelia Webster. She'd died of one of those weird Victorian diseases. Her dad was an artist, but he'd gone bonkers, and done nothing but carve statues of her for the rest of his life. I used to think that was kind of nice. I only saw Dad every other weekend, so if something happened to me, he'd be sad and all, but he'd carry on pretty much the same.

But now I felt for Cordelia's dad. I got why he carved her, why he couldn't get her out of his head.

Because he hadn't been able to save her.

I'd messed up, somehow. What had I missed? I wasn't like, top of the class or anything, but I wasn't that stupid. I dragged myself over to the magpie's door, pushed it open, and went in.

The stiffness dropped from me. I felt myself again.

The sculpture park was impossible. The door should have opened into someone's back yard. Instead, a totally lush lawn spread out in front of me, sculptures all over it, every one of them a human figure. Some were half-finished, faces and arms jutting out of the rough block as if they'd got trapped in the stone. Those ones were creepy, and I avoided them.

The magpie perched on the nearest statue, one of some girl in a really old dress. Even though I felt better here, grief still squeezed at my throat.

"Gran died," I told the bird. "I wasn't even there."

The magpie flapped off, away across the park. Its confidence made me wonder if things could be fixed. Maybe it could like, turn back time. I'd been going back in time in a way, hadn't I? Into people's lives? I mean, it wasn't totally stupid to hope that, was it?

I followed the bird away from the oldest statues at the front. The flash of black wings led me into a part of the garden I hadn't seen. There, the magpie perched on the statue of a familiar girl: Cordelia Webster.

Her head was tilted, and her hair curled onto her shoulders. She crouched down, hand on a chess piece. A board was carved into the base.

The hope inside me chilled. "You just saw me looking at her statue, back in the outside park, right? That's why you brought me to this one."

The magpie nodded, looking pleased with itself. My hands balled into fists.

"But I don't want her. I want Gran. I want her to be alive."

The magpie shook its head.

"They're planning her funeral! I was meant to save her! I promised! I don't want this!"

I swung a hand at the statue, hitting it with a slap. Pain burst through my palm.

Cordelia Webster moved. Her cold fingers grabbed hold of mine. I tried to pull away, but her hands were strong as stone. My heart sped.

"Wait! I need to go back ..."

Cordelia pulled me toward her.

I yanked, trying to get free. "No!"

I stumbled forward, the world tipped up, and I fell into the statue.

I woke in the chair, back in the magical library, myself again. But Chloe's grief lingered. It was too close to my own. I could easily imagine how I'd feel if we had to plan Grandpa's funeral.

"Why didn't Chloe tell me about any of this?"

The magpie gave that funny wing shrug again.

"Well, I need to find her. I need to talk to her, right now."

I hurried out of the magical library.

You should not have shown the girl her cousin's story.

"Why not? Perhaps she could bring Chloe back to me. I still see her pain."

Chloe stole Cordelia Webster from you.

"But Chloe's story is incomplete." There was so much missing from my collection. The people I wanted the most were gone. "Like Isabel's."

You must look to the future, not the past. You simply need more, to ease this loneliness.

"Sometimes it feels not like loneliness. Sometimes it feels like a bottomless hunger."

You would not feel so alone if you listened to me. You have always had the power to take your visitors whole. I know not why you play your ridiculous game.

"I wish for them to choose to stay with me."

Why would they? Your own siblings did not.

I could not argue with that. Even Isabel left me. One day, she'd come to my chamber, cheeks red with excitement. She paced, hands fluttering like butterflies, words coming out in breathless gasps. A strange scent reached me, like the spices of distant lands.

I was afraid she had been taken by fever; for once again the sweating sickness was abroad in the city. But as her words rushed out of her, I discovered her excitement was of another nature.

The son of a wealthy merchant wished to marry her. His father traded in spices and scents. He was charming, and made her laugh. He had brought her gifts of exotic perfumes, captured in jeweled bottles. Our father had approved, and it was settled.

I wished to share her joy, but without her, I would be alone forever.

Once she had gone, The Whisper spoke. "No one will stay unless you bind them to you. You can bring your family together, with your gift and my help."

I was not ready to make that deal.

"You have to end the betrothal, at least," The Whisper said.

I shook my head, but the velvet voice continued.

"Not for your sake. For Isabel's. She is the daughter of a knight. Does not her sweet nature deserve better than a merchant's son?"

I could not argue with that. She deserved to marry a man of name, as Alice had.

The Whisper spoke long into the night, persuading me,

guiding me, helping me make a plan. The following day I disguised my handwriting and wrote a letter to my father, filled with lies to cast doubt upon the character of the merchant's son. It needed but to be sent.

I waited until Isabel and my father were out, and then dragged myself down the back stairs, hands quaking as they traced the limewash of the walls, each breath tight in my lungs. I found a servant in the courtyard, shirking his duties under the guise of a headache. I offered him my silver buckle for his services and his silence. He agreed, for his family needed the money.

When he wiped the sweat from his brow, I thought it was due to his nervousness, like my own. I did not see the mortal fever bright in his eyes, his breath coming too fast.

I handed him the letter. Our hands touched, sealing my fate, leading me here, to this life.

Or this half-life. Whatever it was.

You did not argue so much before this Silva girl came, The Whisper said. *You should take her, whole. For her own sake.*

"That does not feel right."

Trust me. I have always known best.

Chapter Ten

The moment I stepped through the magpie's door and back into the foggy damp of the real world, I regretted it. It felt like I was tearing myself in two.

The wind cut into me, as if my skin had been stripped away and I was a raw nerve. I slipped on the muddy grass and landed on my bum. I sat there as the wet soaked through my jeans. Without the magic of the library to keep it at bay, the exhaustion — the ache of it all — crashed down on me. I didn't want to deal with reality. I yearned for the comfort of the magpie's library.

I stood, wiped myself off, and checked my phone. Mum's message was on the screen.

Fine. We'll have a proper talk when you get home.

I remembered everything. The pills, the tea, the whole reason I'd fled the house. I was too sapped to have a "proper talk" with Mum, or deal with Grandpa's awful disappointment.

I had to speak to Chloe. But what could I say? *Hey, I walked around in your body* probably wouldn't go over well.

I stumbled around the side of the library to the main road, then froze.

The dark figure was there, the person who'd tailed me up the road. The hood of their long black coat covered their face, making them look like the grim reaper. Fine rain misted down.

I ducked back around the corner, heart pounding. Had they seen me? I pressed against the cold wall. They'd followed me up the road, and waited for me. What did they want?

I stood there, breath coming hard, terrified the dark figure would appear from around the corner and grab me. It was only after a few long seconds that I realized I had somewhere to hide. Somewhere they'd never find me.

I crept over the wet grass, reached the magpie's door, and ducked back through it.

Warmth and wellness rushed back into me as the door closed, sealing me in the safety of the magpie's room. I took a deep breath as the magic of the library restored me, making me whole. The gray cloud over my thoughts lifted.

The magpie hopped over. Its tail twitched, as if it were happy to see me back so soon.

"Someone was following me. I have to hide here while I work out what to do, okay?"

The magpie took off and landed on the shelves. It cawed, and tilted its head at the books.

"Thanks, but I don't want to read right now. I just need a moment to think."

I sank down onto the chair in the center of the room. The magpie swooped over and landed on the armrest. I pulled out my phone, planning to call Mum to come and get me. But there was no reception.

"I guess that shouldn't be a surprise. Magic library, no mobile coverage, right?"

The bird nodded at the books again, but I wasn't in the mood to read one. They'd all been creepy or depressing.

"I'm going to wait a bit, okay? In case they saw me. Then I'll make a run for it, over the fence and through the school grounds."

The magpie nodded. I glanced at my phone.

"Do you think ten minutes will be enough?"

The bird gave one of its little shrugs.

"You know what, since I'm stuck here for a bit, can I see Chloe's book? Just to look. I don't want to go into it."

The bird nodded. Chloe's book swooped down into my hands. I turned to the back. The pages there were blank.

"It's not finished. Is that because she's alive?" I shut the book before the letters reached my hands. "And why does it stop there? Chloe's gran died years ago."

The magpie paused, as if thinking. It lifted its chin and turned until its back was to me.

"What are you doing?"

The magpie stood there, beak up, looking away. It was miming something. It stamped its little feet like a child, sulking. I covered my mouth to stifle a laugh.

"She's … ignoring you?"

The magpie twisted back around and nodded.

"Why?"

Again, that funny little wing shrug.

"Did something happen, in that story she entered, the story of Cordelia Webster?"

A nod.

I knew the statue, of course. But the one in the park on Hayling was just of her head and shoulders, not like the one of Cordelia playing chess Chloe had found in her park.

"Chess … wait. I've seen a chess board here, haven't I?" It took a moment for the memory to click. "The book with the torn-out pages! It had a chess set on its cover!"

I rushed to where I'd found the vandalized book, reached up, and pulled it out. There, in the only scrap left of the picture was a chess set.

The magpie still perched on the chair. "Did Chloe destroy this book?"

It nodded, sadly.

"So you won't let her back in?"

The bird shook its head, firmly.

"Is her sculpture garden still there?"

Another nod.

I'd check in the park on the way home, but I was starting to understand, starting to feel the pattern fall into place. "The library *is* the sculpture garden, in a way, isn't it?"

A fierce nod and an excited flutter of feathers.

"It's behind the same door," I waved a hand at the wooden entrance. "Just like the dollhouse and the cinema. Does this place change, according to what we want?"

The magpie was hopping with excitement.

It made sense. I loved books. Margaret loved dolls. Beth wanted to see a film. Mum said Chloe liked to carve and sculpt. This place shaped itself for us, for our passions and desires.

"So, you made this library just for me?"

The magpie looked proud now. It preened, stretching its wings out and lifting its beak.

That explained why I'd seen the girl with the sores as a doll in Margaret's story and a cinema poster in Beth's. Why there was a statue of Cordelia Webster in Chloe's park, but a book in my library. Why each of us had gone through the same door, but found ourselves in a different place. Books, dolls, statues, films: the same stories, in different forms.

I walked over to the chair, and offered my hand. The bird climbed onto my thumb, and I stroked its smooth feathers. It closed its eyes, as if in bliss.

"But why are the stories so sad? Why did you make this place? What's it for?"

The magpie paused at this, the black bead of its eye fixed on mine. It hopped off my hand, and with a quick swoop flew to where one of the roots met the wall. There, on the lowest shelf, was a single book, bound in old leather.

With a rustle like the breeze through autumn leaves, the book quivered and opened its pages. With gentle flaps, it eased itself from the ground, and wheeled around the room once, slowly, almost mournfully, before coming to land on the palms of my waiting hands, weighing them down.

It was the old book I'd picked up first, with a girl in what looked like a dress from a Shakespearean play. If it wasn't a costume, this story had to be almost five hundred years old.

"I can't read this. It's all in italics."

The magpie nodded at it, emphatically.

I leafed through. Much of the book was blank, but the girl couldn't still be alive. I turned back to the crowded handwriting at the start. Was the first letter an 'f', a 'j' or an 'i'? The text was already moving. Could I be pulled into a book I couldn't read? I squinted at the first word.

Jcabal? Fsebil?

The letters reached my hands. The words spread over my fingers. But I should go. Mum would worry. I tried to close the book, but it stuck to my hands with a webbing of words.

THE MAGPIE'S LIBRARY ᔕ 115

"Can you stop it doing that?" I swiped at the letters with the fingers I had free, rubbed at them on my skin, but they tangled, tying me tighter to the book.

"Please? I need to go home."

I strained against the tug, trying to yank my hands away as the book drew me toward the now-blank page.

"No! Please!"

Right before I was dragged in, the first word settled on the back of my hand. The letters spread out, and I could finally read it.

Isabel. It said Isabel.

A baby cried in my arms. Its little hands were bunched into fists, its red face crinkled into a grimace. The girl whose body I was in rocked the baby as she paced. She wore a dress of soft wool trimmed with fur, the dress from the cover of the book. Her long skirt rustled against what looked like hay spread over the floor. Her breath came in gasps as she tried to hold her sobs at bay. With each gasp came the smells of the room: wood-smoke, rosemary and a sweeter scent that turned my stomach.

A single candle sat on a wooden table. It barely broke the darkness, and as it flickered, the shadows danced. The windows were shuttered and wind whistled around the outside of the house, like a creature trying to get in. A bed took up much of the room, with a young woman lying in it. There was a whisper as the blankets shifted, and an arm moved.

"Alice!" Isabel hurried over. "Thou art awake!"

My sister must look upon her son. For it shall soon be too late.

"Here." She laid the baby on the bed, next to the young woman's head.

See how he quietens. He knows his mother.

"Nicolas." The word was a croak. The girl on the bed moved her hand to the baby, who clutched at her finger. She smiled. Her face was wet with sweat or tears.

She is too hot. The childbed fever overtakes her.

She was dying, I realized as Isabel's memories took over, as I sank into her story.

The young woman in the bed had just given birth, and now she was dying.

My body quaked, shaken by the grief held tight inside. The midwife said there was naught that could be done. The priest had been, and my dear sister had been given forgiveness for her sins.

"Nicolas. Oh, is he not a fine boy?" Alice's voice was passing weak, barely stronger than the whistle of the wind outside.

"A bonny boy indeed." I stopped, for fear that a sob would smother my words.

"Grieve not, for I shall soon be with my husband. With our brother." I leaned in to catch Alice's words, soft as her breath. "Yet mine heart aches. For what shall become of Nicolas?"

Alice leaned back upon her pillow, her face bright as she beheld her son, as though the light of heaven shone already upon it. The divine gates would surely open to her, and I wondered if it had been so for Maghew.

I could not think that he would be damned, as Father had said. I had believed him to be blessed. Was that not what the stories said of the seventh child of a seventh child? Yet it seemed he was just as subject to the wheel of fortune and the dark scythe of death as any other boy.

My sister exhaled: a long sigh. No inhale came after.

"Alice."

Her eyes were yet open, fixed upon the canopy above her head. She moved not, and turned not her gaze upon her son when he began to cry. Nicolas's keening was a wordless mourning, rising and falling. For he knew the terrible truth afore I did.

"Alice!" I grasped her hand. "Alice!"

She had gone. I fell forward, my head upon her sheets as I wept.

"Alice." Her very name unraveled me, and the grief possessed my body. For a while, it took my voice, my sight, and my reason, and I bellowed like an animal.

Nicolas brought me back to myself, his mourning louder even than my own. His little mouth was a wide "o."

I reined in my sorrow. I should not think of myself at such a time, should not allow Alice's death to undo me, not when her child needed me. I wiped at my face with my foresleeve, then took his small weight into my arms. I tried to smile.

"Dost ... thou wish for a tale?"

I carried the screaming bundle across the room. He had loosened his swaddle, and waved his tiny fists. His eyes were squeezed shut with the misery of infancy.

I laid him gentle upon the rushes of the floor, and unbound the cloth wrapped around his small form, just as I had with Maghew, when I was but a young girl, and he a babe in arms, afore he was locked away from us.

"I shall tell thee of thy mother. Her hair is ..." I glanced at her. "Her hair was the brown of chestnuts, and more than anything, she loved to dance, loved to kick her skirts out as she spun and turned." My voice caught. Yet I would be telling Alice's story for years. I should start it while her soul was close enough to hear.

I re-wrapped the babe, gently holding down his arms as he squirmed against me. He opened his eyes.

"She would dance till she lacked breath and her cheeks glowed. And one day, a handsome knight saw her dancing, and knew he must marry her."

Hand over hand with the cloth, tightening it as Nicolas watched, as his cries quieted.

"He asked her father for her hand, and since the knight was of good name, the match was made, and the families celebrated."

I tried not to think of my Thomas, back in London. I hoped he was safe from the sweating sickness, hoped I would see his kind face again. I tucked in the cloth, turning Nicolas into a worm with a pink face. He would not wiggle out of that. I carried him to the wooden chair.

"But whilst out riding, the knight was thrown by his horse, and he perished." Nicolas gazed at me. I would let him think of his father proudly astride his steed, not suffering for days before his injuries claimed him.

"His beautiful wife was with child. She returned to her family, who were happy to care for her. But the Lord called her too. She left a boy, so that all could remember her." The baby's face blurred to a pink blob as my tears came.

Nicolas waited for more. I knew not how his story was to end.

I had promised Maghew happily ever after in the tales I told him, yet I no longer believed in such fine endings. Who would win Nicolas's wardship? Would they be kind, or cruel? He was so small, so delicate in my arms. I had failed my brother; I had left him to die alone.

I must not fail Nicolas.

"I shall ask Thomas to buy his wardship as a wedding gift," I whispered to Alice. "With the Lord's help, we will raise him."

A soft knock came upon the door. I carried Nicolas over and opened it to the wet nurse. Her hands were at her chin, tying her cap, as if she had but recently awakened.

"I heard his cries," she said. "He needs a feeding." She kept her gaze low, away from my face. She would have heard my weeping, too, for my grief had not been quiet.

"My sister has gone to her rest," my voice quaked. "I shall keep watch over her tonight."

The servant bobbed a curtsy. "I shall tell the master."

She reached for the babe, and I handed Nicolas to her. I closed the door quietly behind them, and turned to my seat by the bed.

Tomorrow Alice would be draped in black cloth. Tomorrow the bells would ring her to her resting place. Tonight, it was my duty to watch over her.

Who watched over Maghew? Such a dark duty should have fallen to me. But could I have borne it? Mayhap I could have passed the time telling him tales. I could have told him how I begged Father to let us share a tutor, but he said Maghew's lessons were not meet for a young lady. That learning Latin and Greek would inflame my stomach towards vice.

I wished I had told Maghew how much I loved him before I left.

The sobs shook my back, and my fingers grew wet with tears.

I was going to ask Maghew if he would live with us at Thomas's estate, where the air would be more healthful. Yet when I saw how he reacted to my betrothal, an internal voice bade me keep quiet, for fear of further vexing him. Thereafter, everything happened apace: Maghew's sickness growing grave just as we heard news of Alice's husband. Then came the hurried journey out to our country house, where Alice met us, heavy with child. We had not had time to grieve our brother when her labor began.

Now there were but five of us left.

A whisper in my head told me Maghew was not gone. I just

had to reach for him, and we would be together. Forever. How I wished to believe it.

The candle guttered and the shadows crowded me, reaching in from the corners of the room. When the flame grew long once more, I was no longer alone.

A magpie stood beside the bed.

I turned to the windows. Yet I knew they were shuttered, and the door was closed.

"What art thou?"

The bird replied not. It gazed on Alice, black eyes glistening as if it mourned her as I did.

It hopped behind the bed. The curtains were closed upon the other side, so I was not able to see where it went. I followed. But the magpie was gone.

A door stood in its place.

I raised a hand to stifle the cry upon my lips. There had been no door within this wall afore now, and certainly not this door. This door belonged in London. I knew it well, although the form of a magpie was newly scorched upon the familiar wood.

I had let this door shut upon my brother, when he had needed me most.

I pushed it open. Had I not dreamt of doing so every night since we left? Yet it did not open into Maghew's bedroom. It did not open into that awful day a few weeks ago. It opened into a room I had never seen before, bare as a monk's cell.

"Maghew?" My voice was a whisper.

The dark mud of the walls was not plastered. It was empty but for a glass vial in the center of the dirt floor and the magpie that perched next to it.

My little magpie.

The bird had much of my brother about him: the brightness within its eyes, its quick, nervous movements. Yet Maghew was gone. His body grew cold within a London grave. His soul should be with the Lord. How could a boy such as him escape the reach of death?

Such power belonged to the cruel things of the world; things that took delight in the agony of mortals, things that drove us apart. This chamber was too dark for the light that had dwelt within my brother.

It was a trap.

A shiver went through me. "Oh Maghew, what hast thou done?"

The bird nodded at the vial, as if it contained the answer. It looked like the herb oils and rosewater that Thomas's family traded in. Like the perfumes he had given me. I stepped closer, until I could see what was upon it, etched into the glass: the image of a magpie.

I knew that to touch it was to put my very soul in peril, yet I had to know the truth. I picked up the vial, and with shaking hands, unstoppered it. The air in the room changed, as if the small flask sucked everything within it.

Before I could cry out, I was dragged into the dark glass.

I found myself back in the library, slumped on the chair in the center.

The branches felt tight around me, keeping me safe from the outside world. I remembered the Tudor room, the cucumber scent of the floor rushes, the warmth of the woodsmoke, and the feel of the clothes. But in spite of all the changes between my time and Isabel's, the emotions were the same: worry, sorrow, grief, loneliness.

I turned to my companion. "Was that you in Isabel's story?"

A little nod.

"How old are you?"

The magpie swept a wing in the direction of the shelves. The meaning was clear. He had been here for as long as the books had.

"Why was Isabel afraid? Why did she call you Maghew?"

The bird shook its head sadly.

"This would be so much easier if you could talk."

Memories of my own life slipped back. Of the figure waiting for me outside the library. Of running out on Mum and Grandpa. Of being drawn into the story before I could tell Mum where I was.

I pulled out my phone: 7:06 p.m. Mum would have called the police by now. There was no message from her, but there wouldn't be, since I had no reception. I hurried to the door and stopped; afraid the dark figure was still on the other side, waiting for me in the night. I had to get somewhere my phone would work.

But the door was magic, wasn't it? And it had moved once already.

"Is it possible to open this door inside Hayling Library, rather than on the outside?"

The magpie twitched its head back toward the books.

"Sorry, I haven't got time. But if I can go into the real library, I'll be safe. I can call Mum and I'll come back tomorrow, okay?"

The magpie's wings slumped slightly, but it hopped to the door. The old wood shimmered like a motorway in a heatwave. Once it was solid again I creaked it open, just an inch, and felt the stale indoor air on my face, smelled the floor polish. I could make out the metal shelves and the spines of books lurking in the dark.

I took a deep breath, pushed the door open, and stepped into the closed library.

Why did you give her Isabel's story?

"She asked about the library, what it was for. I wanted to show her, as best I could."

Silva was kind. Many were entranced by my collection, but they so rarely tarried to talk with me, or touched me, as she did.

Do you know what you are risking?

"She ... felt like a friend."

Silva is not your friend.

"Perhaps she would be, if she knew me. Perhaps she would choose to stay."

Isabel knew you. And even she did not stay.

The Whisper was right, of course.

My sister burst into my bedchamber late on the day I gave the message to the servant. Isabel shoved open the bed curtains and slumped down hard upon the corner of my mattress.

Her face was flushed as if she had been crying. I wondered if my message had reached our father. But there could not have been time for a break to have been made with her betrothed.

"Isabel, how is it with thee?"

"Did you hear of Rafe?" Isabel gasped.

"Rafe?"

"One of the serving boys."

A sickness sank through my stomach. "What ... what news of Rafe?"

Isabel looked up, eyes wide. "He has died."

"Died?"

She nodded, biting upon her lip.

My heart fluttered. "How?"

"'Twas the sweating sickness. It afflicted him with a terrible speed. They say he had but a headache before noon."

I swallowed down the bile that rose within my gullet.

"And, dear brother, that is not all."

"'Tis ... not?"

"Rafe stole from us. Oh, Maghew, look." She put some-thing cold and small in my hand: my silver buckle. I closed my fist around it, afraid my face would betray me. "They found this within his pocket."

"I ... I cannot think how he came by it."

"In faith, 'tis hard to imagine Rafe as a thief. But there is yet more. He carried a letter."

I clutched the buckle tighter. It cut into my hand.

"'Twas addressed to Father, filled with the vilest slander.

Intended to end my betrothal." She wiped at her face with her sleeve. "I was friendly to him, and I knew not that Rafe could write. Mayhap that is why he wished to end the betrothal, as he hoped for my hand himself."

I exhaled as I realized her mistake. "Oh, Isabel. My heart is sorry for his death."

"I thank thee, Maghew." She sniffed. "I shall pray for the Lord's Mercy upon his soul."

"And I, too." I remembered Rafe's face, his eagerness for the buckle, and his hope it would help his family, and I felt discomforted. "Canst ... thou give this to Rafe's mother?" I held out the buckle. "His father died but a short time since and they have need of money. No doubt that is why he took it."

Isabel smiled, warm as a summer's day. She took the buckle and clutched it to her chest.

"Thou art a goodly man, Maghew. I shall ask Father to make some provision for Rafe's mother. Yet now I must take my leave. The sweating sickness has reached our very door. We must pack, for we leave tomorrow. My wedding will be delayed until it is safe to return."

Rafe's death shook me, of course. But my heart rejoiced that Isabel's wedding had been postponed. Much could happen before we returned to the city. Maybe Father would rethink the match. Or perhaps the merchant's son would succumb to the sweat too.

No. Such thoughts were not worthy of a goodly man.

You are not a good man, The Whisper said. *Isabel is wrong.*

If she ever knew the truth, she would not love you.

The Whisper was right. A good man would not steal. A good man would not write the letter Rafe had carried. But perhaps it was not too late. Perhaps I could still be the good man Isabel thought I was.

A good man would confess his crimes, The Whisper said. *And you will not.*

The Whisper was always right.

That night, I thought I was safe. I thought I had won back my sister. But the Lord did not delay in His judgement. My meeting with Rafe brought its own punishment.

The next morning, the fever was upon me.

My linen shift was heavy with sweat, clinging to my chest. I rolled over, and the blanket wrapped me as tight as a swaddled babe. It was Isabel who found me. She pulled back the curtain. I tried to focus on her, through the shivering and burning that consumed me.

"Isabel," my voice was a croak.

She ran from the room, calling for my father.

When he came, his voice sounded like it came from far away, a shore distant from the wretched one I had washed upon. "I shall send for the physician. But Maghew should have no sheets. They will make the sweat worse."

He grabbed the corner of my blanket.

No. Not the blanket. I felt the tokens I'd taken from my siblings tucked in around me. I clutched tight to the fine wool, fingers locked and aching as they gripped. But I was too weak.

Father yanked, unravelling me, exposing me. I heard the soft thuds as my treasures slipped out and fell to the floor. My neck was stiff. I could not twist to see my collection scattered onto the rushes. But I saw the confusion in my sister's eyes. Saw her brow crumple as she stared down at the precious things by her feet.

"This is Elizabeth's bracelet, James's brooch. Oh! My doll," Isabel bent to pick it up, and clutched it to her breast. "You helped me search. You know I missed it."

My father stared at me. His jaw clenched. "You stole from your own family?"

"They are but mementos ... like holy relics." I knew it sounded wrong, even as I said it.

My father's face contorted with disgust. "I will not listen to such blasphemy!" He addressed Isabel. "We have tarried too long already. We must leave the city. The court has already departed."

I wanted to ask how I was to travel, in this state. I could not ride. Perhaps Father would arrange for a litter.

"Will you still call the physician?" Isabel asked. "For Maghew?"

My father strode from the room.

Isabel hesitated, and then crept to the bedside. "Maghew, why did you take our things?"

"I ... wished only to hold something of each of you, so you felt near."

"Thou hadst but to ask, and I would have given thee my poppet."

I tried to swallow, but my throat felt blocked.

Isabel patted my blankets. "Thou keepest thy treasures within thy nest. Like a magpie."

"Isabel, come!" Father's voice boomed into the room. She scurried after him.

Even then, I never thought she would leave me to die alone. But I was wrong.

So perhaps I was wrong about Silva, too. Perhaps The Whisper was right.

I am always right, The Whisper said, snapping me out of my reverie. *Come, it is time to open another door.*

I sighed, and let the bindings of my books dissolve, let the pages fade until only the text was left, a mist of stories, a fog of souls. The gray cloud tightened and shrank, tangling the words together. It grew darker, smaller, until my stories were compressed into the black of my feathers.

I spread my wings, and took to the skies.

Chapter Eleven

As I stepped through the door, pain hit, like my breath being ripped out through my ribs.

I stumbled a few steps into the library, hand over my aching chest. I collapsed against the hard corner of a shelf, wondering why I felt so awful, as if my blood had been drained from me. No, like something deeper, something even more vital had been taken.

It took a moment for my eyes to adjust, for the metal shelves stocked with romances to resolve clearly in front of me, their pink spines gray in the half-light. The soaring roof looked unfamiliar with the strip lights off: a cavernous space, haunted by shadows.

I took deep breaths. Maybe this was what a panic attack felt like. I had been stressed. There was too much to deal with out here: a stalker, Grandpa's illness, the burned kettle, and the pills. In the library, I didn't need to worry. Everything was right.

I yearned to be back in there. To hide, and never come out.

My phone buzzed in my pocket as messages came in from Mum. The first asked when I'd be home, but the second simply said she was glad, and she'd see me later. I wasn't sure what she was glad about, but she hadn't called the police, at least.

I hurried to the front of the library and peered through the window, hands cupped against the cold glass. Cars crawled past, headlights reflecting off the wet road. There was no sign of a dark figure, just my own reflection, pale as a ghost. I didn't need to call Mum. She wasn't worried. And how would I explain how I'd got in the library, when it had been closed all day?

The initial pain of coming through the magpie's door had ebbed, leaving me feeling worn out, crumpled up. Maybe I'd caught Grandpa's infection. I slumped over to a table and collapsed into a chair. All I wanted to do was lay my head down. So I did.

The cool wood against my cheek was calming. I realized I'd felt like this when I'd been Margaret, but I thought it was the tuberculosis. Chloe had felt awful too, and I'd blamed that on grief. I thought the magic of the library kept my exhaustion, my worries at bay.

Maybe I'd got it wrong.

I'd been feeling worse, the more I visited the library. At the start, I thought I'd forgotten something small. But that sense of loss had grown each time I crossed the threshold. Like I'd been losing something essential, something at the very heart of me.

Cold crept under my skin.

Chloe had been into her park four times, like me. Margaret had been in six times, and felt worse than either of us. Grandpa said she'd died the night of her seventh visit.

The door to the magpie's library still lurked in the shadows between the shelves. There were stories about magpies, weren't there? Superstitions.

One for sorrow, Mum had said. That was a rhyme, wasn't it? How did it go?

One for sorrow,
Two for joy,
Three for a girl,
Four for a boy ...

The library's Wi-Fi was still on, so I Googled it, blinking as the bright light of my phone burned itself into my retina. I found the rhyme I knew, but below it was an older version. A version I'd never seen.

One for sorrow,
Two for mirth,
Three for a funeral,
Four for a birth,
Five for heaven,
Six for hell,
Seven's the devil, his own sel'.

I shivered. Isabel thought her brother was special, because he was the seventh child of a seventh child. Margaret died after her seventh visit. Seven kept coming up.

My phone was a comforting rectangle of light in the library. So I kept reading. Magpies were omens of ill fortune or death. Magpies were thieves. Magpies were collectors.

Collectors. The back of my neck prickled.

A library was a collection of books. Margaret's toy house held a collection of dolls. Chloe's park had a collection of statues, and Beth's cinema held a collection of films. The same collection, in different forms. The stories of real people, their feelings, their thoughts: everything that made them who they were.

The library took a little with each visit. Each time I left, I'd lost more of the core of me: my spirit, my soul. It was being stolen, piece by piece, by the magpie's library.

I'd been an idiot. This was never an adventure. Isabel was right.

It was a trap.

Chapter Twelve

Now I knew why I felt like I'd forgotten something every time I'd left the magpie's library. Each time I came out, I'd left part of myself behind, and now I felt as if a large part of my soul was gone, lost, sealed behind the impossible door.

I let my head drop into my hands. My own book must be in there, filling a little more with each visit. I'd asked the magpie if the finished books were dead people. I hadn't thought to ask what had killed them.

When I'd read enough stories, my own book would be complete, my whole soul trapped inside. They'd find my body on the floor of Hayling Library, like they found Margaret's body on the floor of her room.

My gaze was drawn to the door, lurking in the gloom, inviting me back in. Thoughts were trapped in the mist of my head. My book was there, sitting on a shelf. I wanted to see it.

No. I had to get out, before I let my curiosity get the better of me.

I hurried to the emergency exit and shoved the push-bar.

An alarm screeched. It blared through me, shattering my mind into panic.

Crap. Crap. Crap. If my stalker was anywhere near, they'd have heard that. I stumbled into the misty night, around the side of the library, away from the street.

The fence of the infants' school blocked my way. I clambered over, breathing hard, then pitched myself head-first onto the sodden grass on the other side. Fresh bruises grew hot on my hip where the fence had dug in. I fled across the foggy field as the wail of the alarm grew fainter. I found a shadow next to the school, and collapsed onto the damp ground.

I leaned the back of my head against the rough wall. The wind was a quiet hiss, and the traffic rumbled along the main road. Fog ghosted the buildings that huddled at the edge of the field, making them seem like shadowy illusions rather than real homes.

A figure stepped out of the mist consuming the field.

My breath caught. I could scream, but I was far from help: no one would hear. I pushed myself against the wall, hoping they hadn't seen me, hoping to merge with the shadow I sat in. But the figure walked straight toward me, with heavy, careful strides; like a spider, following the thread of its web to a trapped fly.

My heart pounded. I dragged myself to my feet and backed away. The figure mirrored my steps, between me and escape.

Panic hit. I ran, accelerating as fast as I could. I dashed

across the school field. The drag of exhaustion slowed me, like in a nightmare. My legs were shaky, threatening to buckle.

"Silva! Wait!" A girl's voice: a familiar one.

I glanced over my shoulder. Her hood blew back as she chased me, just enough for me to see the stripe of white in her hair: Chloe.

I stopped; rested my hands on my thighs, gulping down air.

Her own breath came hard as she caught up. "We need to talk. This way."

Fury rushed through me. "You totally freaked me out! Why were you following me?"

"Because you've been acting weird. Because I chased a magpie from your lawn. Come on." Chloe didn't wait for a response. She led me to the fence at the back of the field, and we climbed over. I kept a little distance between us. The streetlights cast cones of orange in the damp air: caves of light that we stepped in and out of.

Chloe's shadowed face was as still as a statue as she led me onto a side road littered with bungalows. Chloe stopped at the first house and perched on the edge of low brick wall.

"Sit."

I stayed standing. "I should get home before Mum worries."

"I texted her hours ago. Said we're having a chat about Uncle Chris."

Ah. That explained Mum's message.

The growl of traffic came from Elm Grove, out of sight behind the houses. I could barely look at Chloe. I'd been in her life. Walked around in her body. I'd felt her grief and knew what she'd lost. But those were her thoughts. Her memories. I had no right to them.

"I heard you slam the door earlier and your mum shouting. I followed you up the road, but you vanished. I waited for hours, wondering if I'd got it wrong, until the alarm went off." She raised an eyebrow. "I'm right, aren't I? You went through the magpie's door."

My jaw clenched. "If you knew what I was getting into, why didn't you warn me?"

"Wasn't sure until just now. I can't see your door. No one could see mine, either." She swiped her hair out of her eyes. "How many times have you been in?"

"Four." I swallowed. "Same as you."

Her frown deepened. "How did you know that?"

"I found your book."

"What book?"

"It was a library for me."

"Oh. My *book*." She folded her arms across her chest "Did you read it?"

"Yes." It was hard to find the right words. "I get it, now. I understand more about you."

"You went into my life." She kicked at the tufts of moss bursting out of the cracks in the pavement. "You expect me to thank you for that?"

"No." I sat down next to her, on the wall. "Sorry."

Her shoulders slumped. She shook her head and looked up at the night sky. I watched her, noting the differences between this Chloe and her younger self.

"What's the white stripe from? You didn't have it before."

Her hand went up and touched it. "I dye it. White and black, like a magpie. I was looking for other people who found the door. I thought it might be a clue to help us find each other. But you didn't work it out."

I shook my head, feeling stupid. It hadn't even occurred to me. "So, how do we fix this?"

"We can't."

"What do you mean, we can't?"

She shrugged. "I've felt drained for years. I've had tests, but the doctors couldn't find anything. It's not so bad that you can't function, but it does suck."

"No, that can't be right. I can't be stuck like this."

Chloe's face was dark under the shadow of her hair. "I am."

"Okay, medical stuff wouldn't help, because it's magic. But there must be a magic way to undo it." It felt a bit stupid when I said it out loud.

"There isn't. You've lost part of your soul and you can't get it back. You have to accept that. You only make things worse when you run from the truth."

My jaw set. "It's not running. It's trying to do something. Get back the piece we've lost."

"You can't go back in there. It'll kill you."

"I can't live like this!"

Chloe's eyes glinted in the streetlights. "You have to. I have."

I couldn't believe she could be so passive. "You've dealt with this for what, five years, and that's your brilliant plan? I'm not giving up that easily."

"You think I gave up easily?" Her voice trembled.

I stood. It felt contagious: her flatness, her inability to fight. I had to get away. Had to think it through on my own. "I'm going home."

She shouted after me. "You have to face reality, Silva, or you'll die."

I sped up, hurrying away from the pain of her words. Cold fingers of wind reached in through the gaps in my clothes, and I wrapped my arms tightly around myself.

I turned onto Elm Grove and checked over my shoulder, expecting her to follow. The lit windows of houses shone gold as I passed, inviting and warm against the cold night, reminding me of the shining dust motes of the magpie's library. It was only when I was almost home that I realized why Chloe hadn't followed; why she took a different route to get foot powder, why she wouldn't buy Persil at the shop on the corner.

She was avoiding the park. She didn't trust herself to go near her door.

She wanted to go back in, too.

Breakfast the next morning was awkward. I couldn't tell if Grandpa had forgotten about the pills, or didn't want to bring them up. Hollowness rang through me, and I desperately wanted to fill it. Mum made bacon and eggs, and I ate and ate, but at the end, I felt sick and bloated. The soul-hunger remained.

The third time Grandpa commented on the rain, Ollie carried his plate into the front room. Mum stood, and put her hand on Grandpa's forehead.

He pushed it away. "Stop doing that, Ruthie."

"Sorry," Mum said. Neither of us reminded him of Mum's real name.

I tried to concentrate, to think of something that could help, anything except going back to the library, but my thoughts were as hard to clutch as smoke.

Mum sat with an exhausted exhalation. "How did your talk go with Chloe?"

Grandpa lifted his head. "You've been talking? About time you worked out whatever came between you two. When we first moved here, you were like sisters."

"Chloe," Mum corrected him. "It was Chloe and Silva, not me and Janet."

Grandpa nodded, but his gaze stayed fixed on Mum, his brows furrowed.

Mum sighed. "Doesn't matter. It's time for us to head to the doctor's."

Somehow, I managed to get showered and dressed, and threw my stuff into a gym bag. My world was collapsing, yet I was meant to go back to Bedford today, back to school tomorrow.

I picked up my bag and lugged it down the hall. In Ollie's room, socks and abandoned jeans were strewn over the floor. Anger shot through me.

"Ollie! Pack your mess!"

No answer. I stomped downstairs, loud enough that he would know I was annoyed.

"Ollie! Come on! Mum will be back soon." The kitchen was empty.

"You know what? I don't care! You can be in trouble! Serves you right!"

I hurled my bag onto the ground and stumbled into the front room.

I stood there, staring at the shelves, feeling as if something was wrong.

It took me a moment to put my finger on it. Some of the photos were missing. One of me and Ollie, and the picture of Grandpa and Margaret. I put my hand on the shelf, in the gap where the pictures should be. The click of the front door distracted me.

"We're back!" Mum's voice was too high. Fake cheerful. "Sit down, Dad. I'll make tea."

Grandpa shambled into the kitchen, shoulders slumped.

Mum shut the door. "Did you pack?"

"*I* did, but Ollie ..."

"Best to unpack. Sorry."

"What ... what did the doctor say?"

"Grandpa has a fever."

"The infection's back?"

She rubbed her forehead. "They're not sure if it's the same one. It could be something he picked up in the hospital. There are a lot of sick people there, and sometimes you can catch a virus while being treated for something else. We need to stay, see if he gets better."

The ground felt unsteady. "And if he doesn't?"

"He won't take antibiotics. He's agreed to take his painkillers, and the doctor suggested a higher dose since they're not trying to keep him ..." Mum closed her eyes. A sob escaped. Her hand went to her mouth. I wrapped my arms around her, awkwardly.

She pulled away and wiped her eyes on her sleeve. "I should sit with Dad. Can you make him a cup of tea? Can I trust you to do that?"

"Just tea. I promise."

In the kitchen, I slumped down at the table as I waited for the water to heat in the microwave. My head pounded in time with my pulse, and my mind filled with a sucking emptiness. I stared into space, until a dark rectangle caught my attention, abandoned on the table.

Ollie's phone.

Chapter Thirteen

I picked up Ollie's phone; stared at my face in the black mirror of the screen. My skin was the off-white of old pages; the circles under my eyes dark as smudged ink.

"Mum!"

She hurried into the kitchen. "What is it?"

"Ollie ... his phone was on the table. I was looking for him. He's not here."

The microwave beeped into the silence between us. Mum took the phone and peered at the blank screen, as if it might hold a clue. "Maybe he's gone for another walk."

"Without his phone? Ollie?"

"Could you ... look for him? Check the beach, quickly?"

The beach at the end of the road was empty, so I kept going, pebbles slipping under my feet. The tide was out, the rotting seaweed strung in lines along the high-water mark, filling the air with a fishy stink. I fought through my exhaustion along the shore line, past the frothing waves.

Seagulls took off as I stumbled on, skimming the shingle with wide wings, then wheeling into the air. The chill of the damp wind felt like a razor, slicing through my skin.

I reached the funfair and wandered through the still rides, looming above me, shut down for the autumn. The arcade was still open. A magnet for someone like Ollie. I searched among the candy-colored fruit machines shrieking their tinny tunes and coughing up money with the rhythm of an AK-47. I checked in the sit-in driving games, waited outside the toilets. The noise made my headache worse, but there was no sign of Ollie.

I slumped back to Grandpa's house, worried that I already knew where he was.

Mum stood at the open door, hands clutched together. I shook my head.

"I'm calling the police," she said.

It seemed like a long time before they arrived. Mum sent Grandpa upstairs for a nap and answered their quick-fire questions in the kitchen.

"Has he wandered off before? Have you been fighting? Has he seemed upset?"

They asked about the visit from the Fire Service. They insisted on searching the house, even though I told them I'd already checked. Mum gave them an old photo from her wallet and promised to email a more recent one. Neither of us knew what he'd been wearing, and Mum kept apologizing for that. They asked if he'd talked about harming himself, if he was on medication.

"He probably just forgot his phone," they said. "This happens all the time."

Still, they promised to search, to check the parks and hospitals, see if anyone called anything in, and pass on Ollie's details to other police services. They said if he wasn't back soon, more action would be taken. Then they were gone.

Not two minutes later came the tinny chime of the doorbell. Mum stood so quickly she knocked her chair over. It slammed to the floor with a loud crack. But it was Janet, asking about the police car.

Her prim face dissolved into sympathy as Mum explained.

"I'll get Chloe to drive up and down the island," she said, "check the teen haunts. I'll call my friends, get everyone searching. Don't you worry. We'll find him."

"Thank you so much." Mum clutched Janet's hand.

I'd been putting it off, not wanting to admit the possibility to myself, but there was one place I had to go. One place I hoped I wouldn't find him. One place I wanted to be.

"I'll check in the village, at the shops," I lied.

"Thank you, Silva," Mum said.

The wind was high, flapping my hair around my face. Why hadn't I seen it before? Ollie had spent half his time on Hayling slouching off on his own. He'd probably come to find me at the library and found the door instead.

I stumbled against the fist of wind as it tried to beat me back. Pushed myself along the main road until I finally reached the library. I burst through the entranceway.

Asha looked startled. "Silva? Are you okay?"

"Have you seen my brother?"

"I don't think so. What does he look like?"

"This high. Messy brown hair."

Asha shook her head. "Most children are at school, so I'd have noticed."

Still, I hurried to the door. He could have slipped in without her seeing. I shoved it open and stepped into the magpie's trap.

Just like that, the ache evaporated. It felt like the world coming into focus. I was no longer torn, stretched too thin between two places. I was me.

I took a deep breath, inhaling the golden light, the old-book smell. But there was no Ollie browsing the books, grumpy at me for intruding; just the crammed shelves, filled with the colorful spines of stolen lives, and the magpie, perched on the chair.

It flew to my feet and looked up, tail twitching excitedly.

"You." My voice was cold.

The bird blinked. Its tail lowered.

"You've been taking my soul! You're a thief!"

I was seized by an urge to kick it, to take out the anger that coursed through me. But the magpie flinched at my words. It looked small and vulnerable as I towered over it.

Its skull had felt so fragile when I'd stroked its head, and even now, there was trust in those dark eyes.

"I thought you were ... I thought we were ..." I wanted to say "friends" but that made me feel like more of an idiot. It was a bird.

My hands clenched into fists, and I punched the chair instead. Pain shot through my knuckles. I screamed in frustration. The magpie took off, flying to a high shelf with two books on it. I pressed my palms into my eye sockets and screamed again.

Of course Ollie wasn't here. Ollie wouldn't have seen my door, just like Chloe hadn't. He didn't read much and wouldn't have been tempted by a magical library. I turned toward the exit, bracing myself for the pain of leaving.

But a thought whispered in my head.

A library wouldn't have tempted Ollie, but something else could have. Chloe had her statues. Margaret had a dollhouse. Beth had her cinema. But if Ollie were caught in another form of the magpie's trap, how would I find him? I wouldn't be able to see his door.

Then it hit me.

The collection was the same, no matter what form it took. If Ollie's soul had been stolen, he'd have a book here, one with his picture on the cover. I spun around.

"Is … is Ollie here?"

The magpie nodded at one of the slim volumes it perched next to. The book rustled as it eased itself off the shelf, opened the wings of its pages, and swooped toward me.

A chill spread through my blood.

I held my hands out, and the book bobbed down, like a papery butterfly. It landed face-up on my palms: a glossy, colorful paperback. On the cover, a boy stood in an arcade, the familiar shape of him silhouetted against the light of the games.

Ollie.

The world seemed to tremble, but it was no earthquake. Only I was shaking.

My brother looked too small on the cover. Too young. I swallowed.

"How many times has he been in?"

The bird nodded at the book in my hands. I had to read it to find out. Ollie could be dead already.

No. Please, no.

I opened it to the back. To Ollie's ending. It was blank. I exhaled. I wasn't too late, but there were only a few unwritten pages. I had to find him before he went back in. But there were several arcades on Hayling, and I wouldn't be able to see his door.

"Where is Ollie's trap?"

The magpie ruffled its feathers, as if offended.

I fought the urge to hurl the book at the stupid bird.
But that might hurt Ollie. Instead, I turned to the start
of his story.

*Oliver peered out of the window as the car pulled up at
his grandfather's house. In the front yard weeds choked the
roses and a magpie sat on the overgrown lawn.*

There had been a lot of magpies around lately.

The O wiggled toward my hands.

"One for sorrow," Oliver's mum muttered under her breath.

*He leaned forward, looking for a sign that things would
be okay. Instead he saw the dark rectangle of the open door,
the rain slanting into the house.*

Dread coiled in my stomach as the words inched onto
my skin. This was Ollie's story. It wasn't mine to read,
and I didn't want to lose more of myself.

*A sickly taste filled Oliver's mouth. "Why is the front door
open?"*

Ollie's thoughts spread up my arm. I had to save my
brother. I had to find his door, before he went back in
again. Even if it meant losing more of myself.

*"He's probably waiting for us," Silva said. "Standing back
a bit so he doesn't get wet."*

*Oliver fought the urge to kick the back of his sister's seat.
Why was she pretending everything was normal? Didn't she
see how tense Mum was?*

No. This was a mistake. There had to be another way
to find Ollie. I'd force the magpie to tell me. I'd wring its
little neck.

THE MAGPIE'S LIBRARY ᴄ᷉ 151

I tried to pull my hands away, but the words held me tight as a net, tying me to the book. I yanked, wrenched, pulled as hard as I could, but it was too late.

"That's stupid. He doesn't know we're coming," Oliver snapped.

I cried out as I was pulled through the page and into Ollie's story.

I was in Ollie's body, in the back of the car, staring at Mum in the front. Staring at the back of my own head. I wanted to lean forward to warn myself.

But this wasn't my story.

"Well, come on then," Mum said.

I don't want to go in the house. Who knows what we'll find?

Mum and I opened our doors and hurried into the rain. Ollie followed slowly, making no attempt to stop the water running through his hair, over his face. It was weird. I was there, sprinting through the rain in front of him, but I was here, too, watching myself through Ollie's eyes. It made me dizzy.

It was a relief when Ollie's thoughts pressed in, crowding out my own feelings, replacing them with his.

The door was a black hole, and its gravity pulled me in. Water dripped in my eyes. I shook my head and caught the smell of rotten food.

"Maybe he popped out," Silva said.

What was wrong with her? Why did she always have to be Little Miss Cheerful?

"In this rain? And what about the post?"

My clueless sister noticed the mess under her feet for the first time.

Mum looked around. "I thought Chloe was cleaning for him."

"Then Chloe's doing a rubbish job," I said. But it felt wrong. Stupid words muttered to try to fill the gap between how things were and how they should be. No one listened anyway. They never did.

"Perhaps I should check on my own." Mum's face was grim. "Perhaps you two should wait outside."

I knew what she was afraid of finding: Grandpa's body. I leaned against the wall, trying to breathe. My vision blurred. "Fine," I managed. "I'll be in the car."

I stumbled out, not feeling the downpour, just the fear like a football in my gut. I yanked the car door open, dove in, and slammed it shut. The rain fell on the roof, a background growl.

Breathe, breathe. Out, in. Try not to stress about it. Try not to imagine Grandpa, eyes open and blank, body cold and stiff.

My breaths caught in my throat and mutated into sobs. I cried. Like a baby. Like an idiot. Big, wet, gulping gasps for air. I hid my face in my hands, ashamed.

It was a long while before I got it under control. I wiped

my eyes on my sleeve, and saw Mum running from the house, Silva right behind her. I pulled my phone out and stared down at it, so they couldn't see my stupid red face. The car rocked as they climbed in.

"He's in hospital," Mum said. "We're going to see him now."

There was hope again. Tight in my chest. Almost as painful as the fear.

At the hospital, Grandpa didn't recognize us. I made up some excuse and got out of the ward before I cried again. I spotted the wheelchair and slumped down hard into it. People stared as they passed. I couldn't deal with any of it: the people, the place, the fluorescent lighting.

The antiseptic reek reminded me of vomit, I guess because Mum always used antiseptic to clean up after we'd been sick. I worried it would make me puke right there, in front of everyone.

I pulled out my phone to choose an app — something to help me keep it together. My finger hovered over the FIFA one, but it reminded me of my freak-out on the pitch in Bedford. I opened Peggle instead.

Play the game. Don't think.

But I couldn't focus, and messed it all up, just like everything. The balls slipped off the edge of the screen.

Game over.

Silva came stomping down the corridor like the whole thing was my fault. She buzzed around, irritating as a wasp.

Dragged me to my feet and back to the ward, where Mum was deep in one of her stupid fights with her cousin. I tuned most of it out.

Mum sighed. "We need to take care of your grandfather."

"Wouldn't the hospital be better for that?" I said. No one looked at me.

They never listen, a voice in my head pointed out. It's like you're not even there.

Mum pinched the bridge of her nose. "Look. Let's get in the car. There's something I should have told you two. Something we should talk about in private."

But I already knew what it was. Grandpa was dying.

Silva insisted on going to the library on the way home. I thought about going with her, but she gave me a funny look when I was about to ask, and I knew, as sure as if someone had whispered it in my ear, that she didn't want me there. She was fed up with me, like everyone else. Anyway, she'd probably skip around like everything was fine, sticking that fake smile of hers on.

I asked Mum to drop me off at the beach instead, saying I needed some fresh air. She pulled into the car park by the boarded-up ice-cream place.

"It's pouring. Are you sure?"

"Yeah."

She twisted around in her seat. "Are you okay, Ollie?"

"Yeah."

She stared at me for a long moment. "You don't want to go back to the house while it's a mess, is that it?"

I nodded.

Mum dug into her purse, pulled out a tenner, and passed it to me.

"Get some food at the funfair. At least there you'll be out of the rain. I'll sort the house as quickly as I can."

I got out and stumbled through the gorse to the shoreline. The rain spat down on me, driven sideways by the wind. But I had the beach to myself.

I shouted as loud as I could, swearing at the sea. The noise was swallowed by the rain, the gray waves smashing on the shore. No one could laugh at me for crying here, like when I lost it when I was trying to get on the football team in Bedford. I scooped up handfuls of stones and wet clumps of sand and flung them at the sea so hard my arm muscles ached.

The anger faded, slowly replaced by a numb exhaustion. Just a few days ago, I'd thought it might be better if there was a reason for this stupid feeling, for this angry sadness, like a weight squishing me into the ground. Now I had a reason, and it just made things worse.

I wandered along the shore, thinking about how we used to collect driftwood here with Grandpa. He taught us army chants and how to bounce flat rocks on the waves.

But those days were gone and would never come back.

Small cliffs of pebbles crumbled as I stepped on them,

making me slip. When I looked up, I was almost at the fun-fair. A rumble in my stomach reminded me of the money Mum had given me.

I hurried in through the side gate. The rides were shut down for the season, skeletal rails spiraling into the angry gray sky. Carriages slumped under blue tarpaulins that snapped in the wind. But the arcade was open, and it glowed. I yanked open the double-doors and stumbled into the warmth beyond.

I tried to wipe my face, but my hands were wet and so cold they didn't feel like a part of me. Lights flashed and spun, leaving loops burned in the backs of my eyes. I clutched the money in my pocket. I should spend it on food, but maybe I'd have enough for a few games, too.

I watched the demo mode on the machines. Men fought. Zombies lurched. Cars raced. But they were all old, with rubbish graphics and high prices.

That's when I saw the magpie again.

It didn't seem bothered by the noise and the lights. It watched me for a bit, and then hopped into the small space between the wall and a row of basketball games. I followed, and peered into the gap. It was a couple of feet wide and filled with electrical cables.

But there was no bird there.

Maybe it had got stuck under a machine, tangled in the wires. It could hurt itself, stupid thing. I stepped over the nearest adapter and squeezed into the gap. Still no sign of the magpie. But there was something set into the wall.

A door.

I shuffled farther in, turned sideways until I stood right in front of it, the wood a few inches from my nose. It was well old and the outline of a magpie was burned onto it. No handle and no lock, but when I pushed against it, it swung open easily.

I stepped into the room on the other side, and my jaw dropped.

It was a huge circular arcade, lit by the glow of hundreds of games. Floor after floor rose above me, each reached by a tangled system of staircases painted in UV, swirling around a central foyer. Flashing LEDs cast multicolored light onto dark walls.

The magpie perched on a handrail, right at the top.

It was way better than the arcade I'd just left. This was my idea of heaven. But could I afford it? I peered at the nearest game to see how much it cost.

There was a boy on the screen. The graphics were top notch, hardly pixelated at all. It was in demo mode, and he walked toward a model village on a bright, sunny day. There were no coin slots, but words flashed in the upper right corner of the screen: PRESS START. So there had to be credits in the machine already. Nice.

My hands slipped into place on the old-school control panel. I hit the red start button, and squeezed the joystick tightly, wondering if this was a scrolling platformer.

Instead of the game starting, the pixels jolted down the

screen, as if the image were crumbling into bright dust. Scraps of light fell, a fragment at a time, leaving black at the top of the monitor. And, impossibly, they tumbled out of the frame and flowed over the controller.

The light danced onto my fingertips, settling over the back of my hands. I was too shocked to move, too shocked to breathe, watching the light pour out: all different colors, on my wrists, then my arms, making them shine. The pixels spread until my skin was alight and the monitor was black. The screen rippled like the surface of an oil slick.

The lights on my arms tightened and pulled me into the darkness.

I woke on the floor of the magpie's library, in my own body. I jumped to my feet and ran for the door.

I knew where to find Ollie. I hoped I wasn't too late.

The girl's motes sparkled in the air, yet I felt no joy at the beautiful part of her she had left.

She had been so angry with me.

I told you, The Whisper said. *You should not have shown her Isabel's story. You should have listened to me.*

"I ... thought she might understand."

I am the only one who understands. Gather what she has left. We need to keep her safe.

"She does not wish to stay in my collection. She was afraid."

She is but a mortal, and what do they know? How many lives have you seen flare and fade, brief as a rush light? Remember how you almost perished? Would you wish such an end upon her?

A shudder went through my wings. I would have died without The Whisper. It saved me when the pain of the

sweating sickness grew too much on that awful day hundreds
of years ago, when my father and Isabel found my stolen
treasures and left me to die. The Whisper had kept its
promise. The moment I made the deal it pushed out the
disease, pushed out the agony of my neck, my shoulders,
the weakness of my body. It filled the cracks in me, settling
under my skin like dark armor. I stretched, my arms moving
easily. They opened and spread, feathered and dark.

I flapped my new wings and rose away from the still figure
on my bed. I rose through the stone, up through the ceiling.
I rode the updrafts of the city.

My house shrank, merged with the higgledy-piggledy
rooftops. I wheeled around, watching the world below.
Between the buildings, the streets of London twisted and
zig-zagged, people crowding along the narrow passageways,
on foot and on horses.

I saw the people, saw their clothes and their faces: dirty
and clean, desperate and proud. I saw the trails they left,
like blood in water, staining the air as they walked. Some
left joy in their wake, some left excitement, or threads of
hope. But a few of the trails reeked of hurt like a bruise in
the air, a spot that it hurt to touch. Their pain drew me to
them, and I felt a desire to pull their sparkling souls from the
fog each of them walked in. I wanted to hold that treasure,
clear and dazzling, free of the dirt and mess of everyday life.
I wanted to keep it safe.

I flew to find my siblings, to save them from their pain.
I went first to Elizabeth and James. Yet the clouds they

walked within were not stained with hurt. Elizabeth was immersed in care for her children and paid no mind to the bird upon her windowsill. James strode past me within the corridors of my father's northern manor, confidence radiating from him. Edmund and Eleanor's trails were not joyful, yet not painful. They were too busy to notice a solitary magpie.

I was too late for Alice. She had already died, giving birth to a son. I'd left Isabel to last, afraid she would ignore me too, but grief and loneliness lay upon her very soul, dark as a tempest.

The Whisper told me what to do. Told me how to make a reliquary, one more secure than my blankets. It taught me how to use my gift to carve a space within the air, a quiet place where Isabel could follow, where we could tarry together.

I stretched, pulled and twisted at the warp and weft of the world, in the same way I had moved the wall hangings and the floor reeds, the same way I had clutched hold of Lettie. The Whisper lent me strength, filling the gaps in my gift, pushing it further, stretching the bounds of nature to make my sanctuary: a home for souls, a place safe from the burdens of life.

My sister was much amazed. I sought to comfort her. Remembering the perfumes she loved, I offered her the only thing I had: myself, my own soul, formed in the shape of a vial. I hoped that she would see me, would know me, and would love me.

When she went back into the world, Isabel left a little of herself with me, and I clutched it tight. It was a true holy relic. It made me stronger, and I waited for her to return, for her to stay, for us to be together.

But she never came back. She married her merchant. They raised Alice's child and more of their own. The years passed, and although I appeared to my siblings many times, none came with me again. Instead, one by one, they followed Alice to the grave. Isabel went to her rest last of all, leaving only the scrap of her that I held tightly.

I never forgot my family. Never lost my longing to be with them. I offered my story to the children of my siblings, their grandchildren, and their great-grandchildren. I shaped myself to match that which they loved. I offered them sanctuary, as I had to Isabel. I offered them escape.

Among my brothers and sisters' descendants, I found those who had need of me: a boy, pursued by wolves; a girl, awaiting her trip to the gallows for taking a few coins from a rich man's pocket. I found those with no way out. They too left relics for me, parts of themselves I could clutch tightly; that I could offer to the others that visited my sanctuary.

Some returned many times. I was able to collect all that they were. I was able to keep them with me, away from the pain of life. Over the centuries, my nest swelled, feathered with glittering souls who lit up the dark space. It grew beautiful, beguiling.

My work went not without notice. The stories began: tales of magpies as harbingers of death, as bad luck. The rhyme was written, the rhyme that would haunt me, would follow me, whispered by those I tried to save.

One for sorrow.

Yet in spite of all my souls, I was alone.

No matter how many of my family I reached, how often they followed me, naught could ease my loneliness. They settled within my collection, as beautiful and separate as jewels. I could but admire them from the outside.

Silva looked a little like my sister, in spite of the generations between them. She understood the importance of family. She had been trying to keep her kin with her, just like me. I wish I could have collected her grandfather, but although I appeared to him many times, he had never followed me.

What is a brief span upon the Earth compared to the eternity you can offer?

"She will not return. She was so angry."

And if she does? Was I not right about showing her Isabel's story?

"I ... yes, you were right."

Would you enjoy watching her grow old and weak? Would you like to see her suffer and die?

"No!"

So, you will listen to me?

I paused for a long moment, before nodding. Silva did not deserve to suffer, as I had before The Whisper saved me. The Whisper was right. The Whisper was always right.

If Silva came to my library again, I would keep her.

Chapter Fourteen

As I stepped back into Hayling Library, my soul ripped away, leaving most of me behind the magpie's door.

I stumbled into the nearest shelves. I grabbed hold of them so tight the metal cut into my hands. I tried to focus, tried to fight the feeling that I'd lost too much, this time. That the spark, the essence, the core of me had almost gone.

It took a while to muster enough of myself to straighten up. To stumble out of the aisle. The ache consumed me, a raw exhaustion through my blood. I'd almost reached the entrance when a voice came from behind me.

"You went back in? What's wrong with you?"

I turned. Chloe stood there, a disbelieving look on her face.

It took me a second to find my voice. "I know where Ollie is."

Her face froze. "Oh no."

"His book is unfinished."

"Where's his door?"

"The arcade at the funfair," I said.

"Let's go." She hurried toward the exit. I struggled to keep up.

In the car park, Chloe gestured to her Mum's blue Volkswagen. I got in the passenger seat and Chloe accelerated away from the curb.

"How did you know?"

"Didn't take a genius. Mum said you'd gone to search the village, so I came here and asked the librarian. She hadn't seen you leave. Are you stupid?"

"I didn't know where his door was. I had to read his book."

Chloe's knuckles were white on the wheel. "Going back in there wasn't about finding Ollie. It was about your addiction. You're using the library to escape your problems. You have to quit." Chloe took the corner onto the Seafront too fast.

"I'm not going back in. We're heading up to Bedford soon, anyway."

"I went up north to live with Dad for a bit, because of stuff at school. But after a couple of months, the door appeared near his flat."

I sank back in the seat. "It ... it followed you?"

"Of course. It's a magic trap, Silva. It's not going to stop until it steals your soul."

I wasn't sure what the speed limit was along the Seafront, but we were smashing it. The rollercoaster grew in the windscreen as we approached the funfair. I jolted against my seatbelt as Chloe hit the brakes at the main entrance. The car behind honked.

"Go. I'll dump this in the car park and join you."

I jumped out. The car wheels screeched as Chloe pulled away. I sprinted through the gates, between the still rides, past the frozen bumper cars, and into the warmth of the arcade.

I could see it through Ollie's eyes now. Shooting the baddie, fighting the ninja, driving the car; it was another world to escape into, like books.

I weaved my way around the clatter of the penny pushers, past the bored-looking girl in the booth, through the pinball games and shooting ranges. At the back of the arcade were the basketball games where Ollie had followed the magpie.

My throat was tight. What if he'd gone back in? Was I already too late? I took a deep breath and peered into the narrow gap behind the games.

Among the tangle of the electrical cords lay Ollie's figure. Utterly still.

Chapter Fifteen

"Ollie!"

I tripped over the wires, fell on my hands and knees and crawled to my brother. I shook him. No response. Bile filled my throat. No. I couldn't be too late. No.

I shook him again, and he flopped onto his back. "Ollie, please!"

His chest was moving. Up, and down.

"Ollie!"

His eyelids flickered and opened. "Silva."

"What's going on?" A voice behind me. Peering into the gap was the girl from the change booth, hair pulled into a tight ponytail on top of her pale face. "You're not allowed back here." Her gaze slid to my brother. "Is he okay?"

"I don't know."

"Might've got electrocuted. I'll get help. Don't touch him." She was gone before I could stop her.

Ollie tried to sit, struggling to find somewhere to put his hands in the mess of wires. I held out a hand. He took it, but couldn't pull himself up. I ended up hauling him to his feet. He stumbled out into the main arcade, then collapsed on his knees.

I dropped down next to him. "Ollie, oh Ollie."

"I think I passed out."

"The other arcade weakened you."

He slumped his weight against me and ended up in my lap, my arms around him. My little brother wasn't a moody brat. He was in pain. I should have realized.

His sobs from the story still echoed through my mind. He'd sounded like he did when he was little, when he fell in the playground. When he'd stumble over to me, arms out, knees bloody and cheeks wet with tears and snot. I used to catch him, hold him while he calmed down.

My sweet brother was still here, but he was suffocating in sadness. I wanted so much to tell him everything was going to be okay, but I'd heard enough about depression to know there was a good chance Ollie had it.

"We need to get you home," I said.

"Okay." His voice was tinny, tinged with an electric buzz. His skin was too smooth, like it was computer generated. Why didn't I notice any of this before?

I typed a quick message to Mum. *Found Ollie at the arcade at the funfair.*

My phone vibrated almost immediately. *Is he okay?*

I had to think before I typed. *He's not hurt.*

Thank God. Coming now.

"There you are." Chloe's voice cut through the clamor of the arcade. "How is he?"

"Weak," I said. "I think he's lost more to the magpie's trap than we have."

"The magpie's trap?" Ollie managed. "Is that what that is?" He waved a hand at the gap.

The wall was blank, but Ollie could obviously still see the door. His arcade stood there, waiting for him, and only him. Chloe and I explained the basics. I didn't mention entering his story. I needed to talk to him about that alone.

"I knew it was draining me. I tried to get more sleep, but it didn't help."

"Sleep won't help. It's permanent," Chloe said.

I glared at her. He didn't need her pessimism now.

"I'll always feel like this?"

"Yes," Chloe said.

"I don't know," I said at the same time.

Chloe folded her arms. "You don't help anyone when you try to avoid reality."

"Just … just shut up," I said. "You don't know everything about this."

"I know more than you."

I clenched my teeth. "Let's just get out of here, okay?"

It took a while to get Ollie to his feet, and we supported him as we made our slow way toward the entrance of the arcade.

"Oliver!" Mum pushed through the doors, running over.

People paused in playing their games, watching us.

"Mum …" In spite of everything, Ollie sounded embarrassed.

She threw her arms around him. "Oh, Ollie! I was so worried."

"I'm okay." Ollie's voice was muffled in Mum's shoulder.

She pulled back, held him at arm's length, looking him over. "What happened?"

"He dropped a coin and it rolled behind the machine," I said quickly. "He went after it, but he passed out. Perhaps he hadn't had enough water or something."

Ollie nodded. "I skipped breakfast."

"You had bacon and eggs," Mum said.

Over the clanging and beeping of the arcade came the keen of a siren, growing louder. The main doors opened, and the girl from the booth strode over. Behind her were two paramedics. "I told you not to move him," she said.

"I don't think he needs …"

Mum stepped forward. "He passed out. And he hasn't been himself, lately."

The woman in reflective yellow and green was at Ollie's side with a brisk rustle. "Any medical issues that could have caused this?"

I shuffled back to Chloe as the paramedics grilled Mum on Ollie's medical history.

"What if they ask more questions about Ollie? How are we going to explain this?"

"We don't. No one will believe us."

"You didn't tell anyone?"

"Just my best friend. She told the whole school I was mad." The lights of a fruit machine reflected in Chloe's glistening eyes. "They called me Crazy Chloe and ... and worse things. I had to get out of there. I moved in with Dad for a bit."

A wave of guilt hit me. I'd assumed Chloe was responsible for the "bullying incident," not that she was the victim. "You had to deal with this all on your own?"

Her bottom lip trembled for a second. She bit down on it.

"Well, for better or worse, you're not alone now." I put my hand on her shoulder.

She didn't move for a long time, then she lifted her own hand up to mine and grasped it, tightly. We stood together, watching the paramedics. One of them checked Ollie's pulse.

"How is he?" Mum asked.

"Since he lost consciousness it may be best to get him checked out in hospital."

Mum nodded. "Whatever he needs."

The paramedics headed out to the ambulance and came back pushing a metal stretcher. They helped Ollie onto it and wheeled him away, his face peering at us over the red blanket.

Chapter Sixteen

"I hate the smell here," Ollie said as soon as Mum left his bedside to ring Janet.

"I know," I said.

There was no space on the children's ward, so they'd put Ollie in a room full of old people. They said they'd be keeping him overnight for observation. The back of his bed was raised to a sitting position. The irregular beep of machines came from other beds, and the nurse's shoes padded softly around the ward as she took medications to the patients.

I closed the curtain around us and pulled the visitor's chair closer to Ollie's bed with an awkward screech. "I have a confession."

"You went into my game," Ollie said.

"It was a book for me. But yeah."

He stared at the white tiles of the ceiling. "It'd be stupid to be mad at you. I've been going into other people's lives all week. Mind you, I didn't know they were real people until you told me." He tried to keep his face composed but gave it away with a sniff. "Did you get lots of juicy dirt on me?"

"No, Ollie," I took his hand and squeezed it. "I was going to apologize."

"What?"

"I've been a useless sister. I should have been there for you. I should have realized."

"Realized what?"

"That you've been struggling. Finding things so hard. Even before the arcade."

His breath came in an odd kind of gasp as he tried not to cry. He looked down at the white sheets covering his thin body.

My eyes watered too. "You don't have to keep it together, not with me."

His face crumpled. I hugged him as he sobbed. After a while he pulled away.

"It's just life though, right?"

"No. I don't think it is. I think you have depression. How long have you felt like this?"

"Feels like always. But it got tough when we moved to Bedford. I totally bottled it when I was trying to get on the footie team, and ..." He paused and blinked fast. "I lost it on the pitch. Like, full-on cried. Like a baby."

"That's why you haven't been playing football."

He ran a hand over his sheets, smoothing them down. "They laughed at me."

"I wish you'd told me."

"I should be able to deal with not being on the team.

It's no big deal. There's no reason not to be fine. That's why it's so stupid."

"It's not stupid. You need help. And not just from me."

"You mean like a … psychologist?"

"Probably. You should certainly tell Mum."

Ollie bit the inside of his cheek. "But even if I am depressed, doctors can't help with the arcade stuff, can they? It's like … like my batteries are low. And that's for life?"

I tried to think of something to make it better but couldn't.

"I didn't think of it as a trap," Ollie said. "Not really."

"What did you think it was?"

He ran a hand through his messy hair. "At first I thought it was like heaven. But after a few trips, I realized it was a deal."

"A deal?"

Ollie stared at the curtain. "A piece of me, for a little escape. I needed a break. I started thinking it wouldn't be so bad, just letting it all go."

"You wanted to …" I couldn't finish.

Ollie shook his head. "Not really. I mean, I wasn't trying to die. I just felt like everything had to change. My life had to change. Anything was better than staying the same."

I felt sick. "Ollie, how … how many games did you play?"

"Six, I think. Yeah, that's right. Two today."

"You can't go back in. Not even once. Promise me."

He shrugged. "Okay. I mean, we're leaving right? I won't be able to."

My heart pounded. I took his hand, squeezed it. "We ... we're staying for a little bit. Grandpa is sick again. I'm sorry. Promise me you won't go back in."

"Ow."

My nails had cut into his skin. "Sorry." I let go.

Ollie rubbed at the red half-moons I'd left on the back of his hand.

"I'm going to find a way to fix it. To replace what the magpie took. I can't lose you, Ollie. Please, promise."

Mum pulled the curtains open with a gentle clatter. "Janet says Grandpa's sleeping. She sends her love."

The man in the next bed started coughing. A breathless, desperate cough. Ollie lay back on his pillows, looking pale and weak. There had to be a way to reverse this, to save him.

Or sooner or later, he'd go back through his door, and I'd lose him, forever.

The next morning, Mum seemed to sleepwalk through the kitchen: staring at the toaster, jumping when it popped. We practically carried Grandpa downstairs, but he only took two bites of his Marmite crumpet before pushing it away.

"What happened to the kettle?" he nodded at the charred mess on the range.

"Just an accident." Mum fixed me with a searching glare. "I have to go to the hospital to see Ollie. You'll stay here until I'm back, right?"

"Yes," I said, quietly. I wasn't going to mess things up again.

Gin stalked into the kitchen, but when she saw me, she hissed and ran out.

Animals really could tell when someone wasn't right.

After Mum left, I helped Grandpa into the front room, where he sank onto the couch. If there was one thing I'd learned from the library, it was that everyone had a story; everyone had a world within them, a struggle hidden from the eyes of others.

I didn't have to read Grandpa's book to know his story. He'd told me, but I'd been too self-absorbed to listen. Grandpa had been fighting for a long time. Fighting back pain, even before the dementia. He knew he'd lose. The only decision he had left was how to end his fight.

I'd tried to take that away from him.

"Sorry, Grandpa," I said.

"Hmm?" His brows rose.

"For the pills. The tea. You know."

"Oh, that's okay." He patted my hand. He clearly didn't remember any of it. He glanced at the window and frowned. "One for sorrow."

I followed his gaze, and my blood ran cold.

The magpie sat on the windowsill. It raised its foot

THE MAGPIE'S LIBRARY ∽ 177

and scratched at the glass. The screech of its claws put my teeth on edge.

"They're bad luck, aren't they?" Grandpa sniffed. "I kept seeing one after Margaret died, and again after we lost your grandmother."

"Did ... did you ever follow it?"

"No. I can't stand magpies." He shook his head. "They bring back bad memories."

I walked over and banged on the glass. The magpie jumped back, wings flapping, but quickly regained its balance on the windowsill. I yanked the curtains closed, plunging the front room into semi-darkness.

"That won't get rid of it," Grandpa said.

I slumped down on the sofa next to him. "I know."

After a while, Grandpa fell asleep. My thoughts kept swinging back to the library. I had two stories left. There must be a way to help Ollie, to do something to his book to free him. I needed to know more about the magpie's trap, and there was only one person I could ask.

I called Chloe and she let herself in with her own key.

"I need a coffee." She slumped into one of the kitchen chairs.

I filled a mug but paused before I got to the microwave, distracted by the blank white of the fridge door. "Did you take the photos from here?"

"No. Why would I?"

There were usually several pictures there, including

one of Mum, holding me when I was a baby. I shook my head. I had more important things to worry about than missing photos. I put the mug in the microwave. "Ollie's only got one visit left. I'm scared he might go back."

"He probably will."

I clenched my fists. "Could you ... not go to the worst possible thought, just for once?"

"Sorry."

"Look, I found Cordelia Webster's story in the magpie's library. But all the pages had been torn out."

Chloe nodded. "Good."

"How did you do that?"

She scratched at a mark on the table with a black fingernail. "I changed her story."

"You saved her life?"

Chloe looked at me like I was an idiot. "This isn't time travel. I freed her soul."

I swallowed down my disappointment. "How do you free a soul?"

"I made her put down the magic chess pieces and stopped her going into another life."

"You took over her body?"

Chloe nodded. The microwave beeped, but I ignored it.

I remembered forcing Margaret's arms to move, remembered the feeling, like pulling things out of alignment. "But ... couldn't you feel that was wrong?"

"Yup." A smile twitched at her lips. She nodded at

the microwave. "Milk, no sugar."

"Sorry," I ran to get her mug and shoveled the coffee powder into it.

Chloe pushed her black-and-white hair off her forehead. "I was mad at the magpie and I wanted to help the girl."

I paused, milk carton over the mug. "What makes you think you did help?"

"I felt … a release. A surge of gratitude. Cordelia thanked me. She knew."

"Knew what?"

"That she wasn't alone. That someone else was there."

"She could feel you?"

"Not at first. But I kept holding on, which kind of stopped the story. Then she felt me. That was what she wanted, more than anything: to know she wasn't alone. Then she could make a different decision."

I put the mug in front of her. "Thank you. Thank you so much."

"What for?"

"I can pull Ollie out."

Her face reverted to stone. "You can't. He hasn't made the final decision. I changed the end of the girl's story. Ollie isn't at the end of his story yet."

"You're saying I can't save Ollie's soul until he's already dead? What use is that?"

Chloe took a sip of her coffee. "It's no use. I keep telling you, we're stuck like this."

"No. I can't accept that." I slid into my seat and leaned my head in my hands.

"Is he okay?" Chloe said, after a while.

"Who?"

Chloe nodded toward the hallway. Grandpa stood in the hall, his face red.

I jumped to my feet. "Grandpa, how are you? Can I get you a cuppa?"

"I ... I think I need to have a lie down." He leaned against the banister.

"Here, let me help you up the stairs."

"Thank you, um ..."

"Silva," my voice was small when I said it.

"I know. I know. I was just getting to it."

I slid his arm over my shoulder, and he leaned his weight against me, more than I expected, almost pulling me over. His skin was too warm. His breath came fast.

"Chloe!" I tried to keep my voice light. "Can you give us a little hand?"

Between the two of us, we got Grandpa upstairs. We dropped him onto his bed, and he rolled onto his front, eyes closing almost immediately.

"I'll message Mum."

Grandpa seems worse. He's napping now. Should I call the doctor?

The dots appeared almost right away. Mum's reply buzzed through.

Wait for me. They're discharging Ollie. We'll be home within the hour.

"Ollie's coming home."

Chloe sucked in air through her teeth. "You're going to have to keep a close eye on him."

Dread prickled up my back. Chloe was right. Ollie was safe in the hospital. But here, he could sneak off to the arcade. And what about when we were back in Bedford, or Manchester? I couldn't watch him all the time.

Maybe we'd be okay. Mum's job kept us moving. Maybe we'd stay ahead of the door. I wandered to the window, to close the curtains. The day had grown gloomy. Dark clouds spread overhead, like ink through water.

The magpie sat on the lawn, waiting for Ollie to return.

Chapter Seventeen

Mum and Ollie got back in the afternoon, and she called Dr. Hussein, who came over an hour later. Ollie watched telly in the front room. The canned laughter of sitcoms filtered into the kitchen as I stared at the burned kettle, waiting for news.

The front door opened and closed. Mum wandered into the kitchen and collapsed into the chair opposite me.

"What did the doctor say?"

Mum put her head in her hands. "He thinks it's a lung infection, and septicaemia."

"What's septicaemia?"

"It's a serious infection of the blood."

"How ... how serious?"

"It's often fatal without treatment."

I tried to breathe, feeling as if I'd been punched in the stomach. "Is he having treatment?"

"No. Only ... only painkillers."

I dragged my chair over and put an arm around her. She turned to me like a child and buried her head in my shoulder. She clutched at me, and I felt as if I were drowning, so far out to sea that I'd lost all sight of shore.

Mum couldn't fix this. She couldn't even keep it together, and she didn't know how bad things really were. I held her for a long time. It was only when she stopped sobbing and the kitchen was silent that I realized what I wasn't hearing. What I hadn't heard in a while.

The telly.

The panic crackled through me. "Back in a minute." I let go of her. She barely seemed to notice, a lost look in her eyes.

The front room was empty. I didn't bother with my coat, just rushed outside, ready to sprint all the way to the funfair, if I had to. But Ollie sat on the lawn at the edge of the driveway. Relief came in a warm rush.

He didn't look up as I walked over and lowered myself onto the wet ground next to him.

"You're still here." My throat was tight.

"The magpie was on the lawn. I chased it away. It flew off toward the beach. It wanted me to come." He took a trembling breath. "Grandpa's going to die, isn't he? Soon."

I wanted to tell him it would all be fine, but I remembered how angry my "Little Miss Cheerful" act made him. I exhaled. Leaned back on my hands on the sodden lawn.

"Yes. I think he is."

Ollie nodded.

"Things really suck," I said. "Like, they suck more than I ever thought things could suck."

Ollie's eyebrows rose, and he looked at me properly. "Yeah, they really do."

"We've been doing the same thing," I said.

"What?"

"Trying to keep things together. Trying to hide how we really feel."

He gave a dry laugh. "Yeah."

"So let's be honest with each other." I offered my hand. "Deal?"

"Deal." We shook on it, and then sat in silence.

"Aren't you cold?" Ollie asked, after a while.

"Freezing. And I feel like hell."

Ollie smiled properly at that. "Me too. We should go inside." But he shuffled a little closer, instead. "The magpie's going to keep coming, isn't it? Until I follow."

"I'm going to stop it."

"How?"

"I have no idea. But I'm not giving up."

I stared at the sky, at the bruise-colored gaps between the clouds as the evening slipped in. Ollie leaned against me, and I realized how strong he'd been. On the day I'd found him behind the basketball machine, he'd known how much it would hurt to leave the magpie's arcade. But he'd still left and tried to come back to us, instead of choosing one more game.

It was like he'd been holding on as a riptide dragged

him out to sea. I thought he'd shut down, but he was just floating until the drag released him, and he could strike out for shore. All I could do was help him keep his head above water until he was able to swim home himself.

And just like that, an idea appeared in my mind, as clear and as fully-formed as if someone had whispered it in my ear. I didn't have to enter a story. It wouldn't cost me anything. It had to be worth a try.

Tomorrow, as soon as Ollie was watching Grandpa, I'd make an excuse and head out.

The next morning the gusts switched directions as I hurried up Elm Grove. They pushed and pulled, tangling my hair. Seagulls twisted overhead, screaming warnings snatched away by the wind. I felt too fragile, as if the wet breeze could rip me into pieces and blow me away like a newspaper in the gutter.

In the library, I scurried between the shelves. There it was: the ancient door, waiting. A chill ran through me. I shouldn't be going in. But I didn't need to read anything, and if I didn't try, I'd lose Ollie.

I pushed the door gently, and it swung open.

It was good to step back into myself. The pain, the ache of separation vanished. The magpie's library still looked as if it was full of wonder, but now I saw that it was the branches and books that were beautiful. The stone walls were dark and cold, like a prison. It wasn't a sanctuary. It was a monster's lair, decorated with stolen souls.

The door shut behind me, sealing me in the trap, the nest feathered with lost lives.

The magpie sat on the chair. It nodded, as if it had always known I'd come back, sooner or later. I smiled. I didn't want the bird to guess what I was really here for.

"Show me Ollie's story," I said, trying to keep the tremble from my voice.

There was a rustle from a high shelf. The spine tipped toward me, then the book shuffled to the edge, like a baby bird, and spread its pages. It flapped down to my hands.

My idea was simple. So simple I wondered why I hadn't thought of it right away. In Cordelia Webster's book, the pages had been torn from the spine. Without them there was no text, no story, no soul trapped in the library; nothing to be dragged into.

Ollie's book held Ollie's soul, sealed in the pages. So, I'd rip them out, leave only the stumps. I'd take the pages, the words that made up his story, out of the library, out of the trap.

I'd have to be quick. Have to do it before the text had a chance to move, or the magpie realized what I was doing. I flipped the book open. Grabbed a bunch of pages at the top and pulled, yanked, tried to tear them away from the spine. I tugged as hard as I could.

They wouldn't rip.

The letters twitched, began to move.

I changed my grip, keeping my fingers away from the words. I grabbed a single page, pinched it at the top, one hand on the spine, the other wrenching with all my strength. I twisted it. The paper crinkled, but I could no more tear it from the book than I could tear concrete.

The letters were crawling, reaching my fingertips. I slammed it shut, just in time. The magpie watched me, head tilted as if it were mildly curious.

Still holding the book, I ran for the door. If I could get it out of the library, back to Ollie; maybe that would help.

But the book slipped from my hands and flapped away. I chased it, leapt for it, and snatched it out of the air. Once again, I dashed for the door, holding it tightly. Ollie's story strained against my grip, its cover opening, squeezing my fingers apart, letters stirring within, swarming out from the pages, seeking my skin.

I let it go with a yelp, and it flew away. "No!" I reached for it. "Please! He's my brother!"

The magpie's tail twitched. It knew there was nothing I could do. The book swooped over to the chair, and settled onto the cushion, waiting for me to read it.

Blood rushed to my face and my vision darkened. I ran to the chair and snatched Ollie's book. I swung my open palm at the magpie, perched on the arm. I wanted to hurt it, distract it, do something. But I was clumsy with panic and it hopped nimbly aside. I stumbled forward, carried on by the momentum. I fell hard on the stone floor, pain bursting through my knees, my shoulder, and my elbow.

Ollie's book slid from my grasp and hit the floor with a loud crack, like the snap of bone. I crawled forward, ignoring the hot ache where I knew bruises would bloom.

I had to check Ollie's story. What if I'd broken something important, something Ollie needed?

The book lay face-down on the ground, open, as if someone was half-way through reading it. I reached for it in a daze and stopped myself just in time. The letters crawled out, spreading onto the floor, scuttling blindly in all directions, searching for my skin. I jumped back.

"You're trying to trap me. You know I won't read a book. You're cheating!"

The magpie watched, something like pity in its dark eyes.

"I'm not going to touch Ollie's book. I won't go near it."

But what was I going to do? I looked up, to the narrow shelf where Ollie's story had been, at the other book that sat there. I suddenly knew whose it was.

The letters scurried around Ollie's story, but the text didn't move far from the pages, as if tethered to them. I climbed up, using the branches as a ladder, hand over hand.

Ollie's shelf was just under the glass dome. The other book that stood there was a slim paperback too. I pulled it out. Even though I'd been expecting it, the cover was still a shock.

It was me. Me standing in this very library, reaching toward a book on the shelf, smiling.

I wanted to slap her, this girl who was me. The girl preserved in the pages. I wanted to yank the book from her hand and hurl it onto the floor.

Instead, I climbed down, still clutching my book, holding it tightly shut. I checked over my shoulder, but the letters from Ollie's story swarmed in a tight circle around it.

Could I go into my own story? Pull myself out? I opened the book at a random page.

Silva's mum twisted around in the seat. "Ollie, are you going with Silva?"

Ollie glanced up from his phone and Silva considered asking him to come. But a voice in her head told her it was pointless, even if he came, he'd only sulk.

Guilt clenched my stomach tight. I slammed the book closed.

I should have asked Ollie to come with me that day. I'd been such an idiot. And I was being an idiot now. Chloe was right. I should be at home with Ollie and Grandpa. I'd been looking for excuses to come back here, to escape my fears and feel whole again.

If only I'd spent more time with my family, none of this would have happened. If only I'd invited Ollie to the library, he'd never have found the arcade. I shouldn't have listened to the voice in my head that said he wouldn't want to go.

The voice in my head. That thought caught, snagged in my mind. It was important, I knew. I ignored an itch in my ankle as I tried to follow the logic. Something about the voice in my head. Something about things I'd been telling myself.

But the itch grew into a tickle, as if a spider crept over my foot. I looked down, as realization hit me, cold as ice.

The letters from Ollie's story had stopped pooling around his book. They'd stretched toward me in long thin lines like ants. They crawled over my feet, over my ballet flats. They swarmed on the exposed flesh between my jeans and shoes.

I screamed, and jumped backward, but the letters stayed stuck to me, wrapped around my ankles, tying me to the page. I jerked away, pulling the strings of text, and the motion flipped Ollie's book over. The pages cleared as the letters marched onto my skin.

I tried to scrape the words from my ankles with my nails, but they wouldn't budge. I scratched harder, flinching as I drew blood, but it was too late.

The webbing of words pulled, dragging me into Ollie's book.

Chapter Eighteen

I was back in Ollie's body, this time on the floor of Ollie's arcade. Games beeped and chattered. Ollie's emotions pressed in on me, his worry and his sadness. I tried to keep myself apart, tried to remember who I was.

I hadn't wanted to be sucked into his story, but now I was here, maybe I could help.

Ollie's memories slipped in. He'd snuck out while Grandpa was at the doctors, desperate for the relief of the arcade before we left for Bedford. He'd just come out of one story.

Do I have time to pick another? They might be wondering where I am.

This was yesterday. I was out there somewhere, looking for him.

Ollie gazed at the games. The tunes were grating and tinny, even to him.

I thought this place was magical, at first. Heaven. I'm so stupid.

The lights he'd seen as glowing and warm flickered like a gaudy nightmare, like flames.

This place is hell. When I first came, I wondered if I could afford a game. He gave an odd laugh. *And I can't. The cost is too high.*

For a moment, I thought he might leave. But he'd told me he played two games that day, before I found him collapsed behind the basketball hoops. I could try to stop him, like Chloe had with Cordelia Webster. Perhaps I could pull a seventh of his soul out. It might help.

My life sucks. My family can't stand me. They'd be better off without me. I might as well play another game.

That thought felt wrong, like an off-key note. It didn't fit in Ollie's head, yet it sounded familiar. I was trying to put my finger on why, but Ollie had made his mind up. He headed for the nearest machine.

Time for me to act.

Chloe said she'd taken over Cordelia Webster's body and stopped her choosing another chess piece. I had to stop Ollie playing another game. I reached into him. Felt his muscles as my muscles, like with Margaret. I willed myself into his arms, his legs, and tried to move them.

Nothing happened.

I tried to close my eyes, but I couldn't. I pulled, I tugged. I threw every part of me into moving my brother. It didn't work.

He reached for the machine, barely checking to see what the game was.

It doesn't matter. Nothing matters.

As soon as Ollie slapped the button, the image crumbled. Pixels cascaded out from the machine, a rainbow of light trickling onto Ollie's hands, working their way up his arms. They clutched him in their glow and pulled him forward, into the now-black screen.

I woke in my own body on the cold floor of the magpie's library.

Of course I couldn't change Ollie's story. Chloe was right. As long as he was alive, he was in control of his own destiny. He was the only one who could write a new ending.

There was nothing I could do for him.

I sobbed on the dark stone. I didn't want to face the wrenching pain waiting for me on the other side of the door. I didn't want to face Ollie and tell him I'd failed.

Slowly, sounds filtered through to me. I stopped crying to listen. They were soft whispering sounds, like paper blown in the wind. I sat up. Books tipped from their branches and swooped to the floor, where they landed with a quiet rustle. Letters spilled from them like coffee from a cracked cup.

I stumbled to my feet, fear breaking over me like an icy wave.

The magpie sat on a high shelf, watching as sentences spread like wet shadows across the stone, oozing into the space in front of the door. The books dove from their shelves, exposing the branches, twisted into unnatural shapes. Stories sailed down, landing in heaps on the ground. Letters scuttled toward me from all sides.

There was no way out of the fast-shrinking circle.

The words advanced. My breath came fast. I scrambled onto the chair in the middle of the room. I cursed as the seat wobbled, afraid it would tip.

"Don't do this!"

The magpie shook its dark head, sadly.

My mouth was dry. "I don't want to go into another story! I want to go home!"

The magpie looked away, as if it were ashamed.

I tried to think. Tried to force my brain to focus through the screaming panic, through the gallop of my pulse in my ears.

The shelves were empty now, the books lying in heaps.

"Why are you doing this?" No answer from the bird.

It wanted my soul, obviously. But it could have done this on my first visit. Could have trapped me right away, stopped me leaving like it was now. Perhaps it had just been playing with me the whole time.

No, that didn't make sense. It couldn't have known I'd come back.

My vision narrowed, focused on the magpie perched on a high branch. Its head hung, as if in shame. It didn't meet my gaze as the words advanced.

Asha popped into my mind. It took a moment for me to work out why, what my brain was trying to tell me. She'd offered to recommend books I'd enjoy. She'd found me the ones I'd needed, put them right in front of me, just like the magpie had.

My knuckles were white against the old wood.

Was the magpie a librarian, in a way? It brought me a book with Grandpa in it, when I'd spoken about him. It had shown me Chloe and given me Ollie's story. It seemed proud of its collection. Excited to bring me books.

The noose of words continued to tighten.

"Please stop!" My voice was high with panic. The skittering black text reached the bottom of the chair. The letters crawled up the wooden legs like spiders, toward my feet. I shuffled away from them and the chair wobbled.

The magpie had offered stories it thought I'd like. Did it want me to enjoy its collection, even as it killed me?

"Let me pick one!"

The words paused. The magpie twitched its head to look at me, as if considering. The whole of the library floor was soaked in letters.

I clutched the chair tighter. "Let me choose my last story. Something I want to read."

Silence fell for a few seconds. Then a whispering noise filled the room as the black tangle of letters retreated from the chair legs. The circle widened, exposing a small patch of dark stone. Just enough to let me sit down. Not enough to let me escape.

The bird and I understood each other.

I couldn't choose to live. I could only choose the last book I'd ever read. I could go into one more story, and then I would die.

I slumped down on the chair, shaking. I put my head in my hands and listened to my quavering breath. I didn't want someone else's life. I wanted my own. I wanted my life so badly it hurt. I wanted my sweet brother and my mum and my stupid moving-around life. I wanted my wonderful grandpa, for the little time he had left.

I'd messed it all up. I let out a shuddering sob.

I'd come to the library looking for escape, and I'd found it. I'd escaped my whole life. They'd find my body on the floor of Hayling Library, like they'd found Margaret's in the sanatorium. My soul would be trapped forever in this nightmare. I wouldn't be able to stop Ollie going back. He'd die. Grandpa would die, too, and it was all my fault.

This was hell, just like Ollie had thought in his story. Heaven turned to hell.

I froze, feeling the words echo through my mind, resonating with a memory.

Heaven. Hell. Heaven, hell.

Five for heaven, six for hell.

The old rhyme. How did it go?

One for sorrow, two for mirth,

Three for a funeral, four for a birth

Five for heaven, six for hell.

A prickle ran up my spine. Seven magpies. Seven books before I lost my soul. Margaret was consumed with sorrow. Mirth had punctuated Beth's story: hers and her cousin's giggles, on their way to see a comedy, before Emma had laughed at them. Chloe's family was planning her grandmother's funeral, and Alice died giving birth. The first time I'd gone into Ollie's story, he thought his arcade was heaven. But on my next visit, it had become his hell. Six stories: sorrow, mirth, funeral, birth, heaven and hell. What was the last line?

Seven's the devil, his own sel'.

I shivered. This was all about magpies: the rhyme; a magpie on our lawn; a magpie leading us to the trap; a magpie scorched on the door; and a magpie on a vial, in Isabel's story.

I froze, my trembling hands still for a second.

I'd asked the magpie why it had made the library. It had shown me Isabel's story, where there was only one object in the collection, a vial with a magpie etched into the glass.

My little magpie, Isabel had said, but she'd been thinking of her dead brother.

Could the magpie have been the first soul caught in the trap?

The books were heaped on the floor, letters spread like nets around them. The collection was the same, wasn't it? Dolls, books, games, films, statues. If there was a magpie vial in Isabel's story, there must be a magpie book hidden in the heaps around me. A book I could read. Perhaps even change.

If any story could make a difference, it would be the first. I took a deep breath.

It was time to face the devil himself.

Chapter Nineteen

But where was the magpie's book?

Six roots ran out from under the chair to become the six sections of the library. Which of the sections had the magpie's story been in before the shelves emptied? There were no labels, no clues anywhere, and the books were a mess.

They rustled, pages shivering, the library impatient for me to choose. I closed my eyes and tried to think. Six sections it could be in. Six roots that ran across the floor.

Wait. Six was wrong. It didn't fit.

Seven stories. Seven magpies in the rhyme. Isabel's brother was the seventh child of a seventh child: sisters, brothers, branches and roots. My eyes flew open as it clicked into place.

A family tree. The whole library was a family tree.

It was obvious when I looked around. That's why the oldest books were at the bottom. That's why Ollie and I shared a shelf. That's why all the books I'd read were in the same section of the library, with Isabel's at the bottom.

Isabel was my ancestor.

Six roots, even though Isabel was one of seven siblings. But Isabel's little brother had died when he was too young to have children. His branch of the family tree was a dead end.

Maghew, that was his name. Isabel's little magpie.

The chair was the heart of the library. Six roots came out from under it. Six siblings that had children, grandchildren, and great-grandchildren all the way to the present day.

But one hadn't.

I climbed down and pushed the chair. It moved; just an inch.

The magpie gave a caw, and flew down from its shelf to land next to me.

The chair was heavy, old wood. I leaned all my weight onto it and shoved. It scraped across the floor. Another inch, and another, exposing the center of the roots. Exposing the core, the point where they joined.

And exposing something else with it.

A withered root, running alongside Isabel's, that ended after a few inches. On it laid a little book, no bigger than the palm of my hand, the blue-black of midnight. The outline of a magpie was embossed on the cover, wings clutched against its sides.

The magpie's story.

The heaped books rustled. The whisper of their pages built to a crescendo as I picked the story up. It looked like an ancient notebook. A diary. Slowly, the library grew quiet. The sound hissed out, like a dying flame, leaving the magpie and I in the silence together.

It looked up at me, dark black eyes unreadable. But I got the impression it wanted me to read its story, that it wanted to be known, to be seen, to be understood. It had tried so hard to explain itself to me, with its nods and shrugs, with its little hopping mimes.

The library held its breath. I took the book, sat down, and opened it. My hands trembled.

This is wrong, a whisper in my head said. *Put it back. Pick another.* I ignored it.

This was the right book.

The pages were brittle, and there weren't many. I turned them carefully, afraid they'd crumble at my touch. The words were handwritten, not much more than a scrawl.

"This one," I said.

The magpie sat in front of me like a child waiting to be told a tale.

"I choose your story."

There was sadness in the bird's eyes, dark and deep as a lake. It nodded, once.

I jumped as the letters moved. They scuttled onto my fingers, crab-wise and crooked. I struggled to stay still, wondering if I'd made a terrible mistake. Wondering if I should have listened to the warning in my head. The words scampered over my hands as my heart raced.

I let them settle on me, let them spread over my skin.

The page cleared. The words clutched my arms tight and pulled me into the book.

For a moment, I thought I was in a cupboard with a cushioned floor, and then I realized I was lying in a four-poster bed, the curtains almost closed around me. I was in the sixteenth century again, but I wasn't Isabel this time. Sheets covered my body, topped with embroidered blankets, and one thin arm lay on top of them: Maghew's arm. The air was heavy with woodsmoke and the reek of sweat. Maghew's body was hot with sickness and pain.

There was a small gap in the bed curtains, and I tried to focus on the wider room. It was dark, lit only by a single candle. Colorful wall-hangings decorated the chamber. A door was set into the wall opposite. It was familiar, thick and ancient, but there was no magpie scorched on it.

The agony pushed in on me along with Maghew's memories: memories of being constantly sick and alone, the shame of being caught stealing from his own family. The memories tried to replace mine, but I clung on to myself. Clung to my soul.

If I was going to die, I was going to die as me.

His thoughts were disjointed, and perspiration dripped from his hair into his eyes, blurring the room.

Make the deal with me, a voice in his head said. *And I can end the pain.*

A chill went through me. I knew that voice.

I'd heard it before, in my own head, although I'd thought it was my own. It was the voice that told me not to invite Ollie to the library, the voice that told me not to read Maghew's story. I'd heard it in Ollie's head, too: the voice that told Ollie that Mum and I would be better off without him. In Maghew's head, the voice was louder, impossible to ignore.

I am the only one who cares about you. Listen to me.

It spoke over Maghew's own thoughts, drowning them out. The voice ripped into him, tearing into his lonely soul, and he wept into his pillow.

Isabel will be back soon. She will help; surely she will.

I tried to focus, but the pain drove a wedge between me and my memories. I struggled to stay myself, to stay afloat as the fever tumbled through Maghew's mind, threatening to drag me into the sea-sick depths of his confusion. I was suddenly aware of someone standing above us.

To Maghew, the doctor seemed like a creature from a nightmare, his features elongated into a beak by his plague mask, black robes hanging from his shoulders like wings. He leaned over the bed, and for a moment, Maghew thought he was looking into a mirror.

Magpie: was that not what Isabel had called me?

Maghew's heart raced. The doctor stank of sweat and vinegar, barely masked by the nauseating sweetness of cloves. Pain seared through my head and neck. A weight pressed upon my chest and I struggled to inhale. An overwhelming thirst consumed me. Maghew begged for water, but the doctor had already gone.

It is time, the voice in his head said. *You can bring your family together. Bind them to you, forever. But you must make the deal now.*

This was the decision, the one I had to stop. But Maghew did not want to make it.

No. I must be the goodly man Isabel thinks I am.

The voice kept up its whisper. Kept hissing in his head, trying to persuade Maghew. But he would not agree. After a long time, I was aware of another noise in the room, a different voice.

"We must leave."

Maghew twisted his aching neck. The door was open a crack. A girl peered through. The shock of recognition made me dizzy. I had worn that fur-trimmed dress. Her name came to me, from my own memories, and Maghew's: Isabel.

Her father stood behind her, his hand on her shoulder. "We have many hours to travel before nightfall."

Isabel wiped at her eyes. "May I ... bid him goodbye?"

Maghew pulled in a shuddering breath. *No. They cannot be leaving without me.*

His father's grip tightened on Isabel's shoulder, and she flinched. "We cannot risk breathing the miasma that surrounds him."

Maghew's throat was tight, almost closed with the swelling of his neck. He reached a shaking hand towards his sister, perspiration glistening on his skin.

"Could not the physician help him?" Isabel said.

"He is only God's instrument. The Lord shall decide if Maghew lives or dies."

"The priest?"

"He is busy. This sickness is abroad in many homes."

Tears began to fall, clouding Maghew's vision.

"We cannot leave him, father, please."

"'Tis divine punishment for his thieving nature. We shall pray for him, but the pestilence shall claim us all if we flee not the city now."

Maghew's mouth moved, but no sound came from his parched throat. For a moment, I thought Isabel was going to step into the room, toward her brother.

Their father spoke again. "Naught can be done for him, and Alice has need of thee."

Alice? Wasn't that the dead girl in Isabel's story?

Isabel squeezed her eyes shut. Maghew's father steered her away and the door swung shut behind them. Maghew waited for it to reopen, but it stayed closed.

She cannot have gone. She would not leave me to die alone. She would not.

Maghew stared upon the door, still not believing, and my heart broke.

The sickness grew worse. A hot agony held my limbs rigid, paralyzed with pain. My breath came hard. My gut burned. Maghew was going to die soon, that was clear. He was going to die in this room, abandoned by his family, all alone.

No, not quite alone.

I told you they never loved you. The voice sliced into his aching soul, sharp as a razor. *I am all you have left.*

There was a triumph in the words, in the dark velvet tone. Even through Maghew's pain and confusion, the cruel joy was clear. The voice left a long pause then spoke slowly, like it was savoring the sentence.

I could leave you too.

"Please, do not do that."

The voice did not answer. Silence rang through the room.

"Are you there? Come back!"

The boy's heart sped dangerously fast, the panic leaving him weaker, dizzier.

"I'm sorry! You're all I have!"

Still no answer. Maghew clutched the bedclothes, the panic seizing his breath.

So that was how it had happened. A deal had been made with a dying boy, terrified and alone. A deal for his soul. The pain within Maghew hardened, resolving itself into a dark determination.

The priest will not come to take my confession. I will die unforgiven, damned to hell. If I am damned, what do I have to lose? Was there not meant to be a price for a soul? Am I not owed more than a lonely and painful death? Is it so wrong to wish to live, to be with the people I love?

"I'll make the deal! I don't want to die!" Maghew said.

Finally, the voice spoke again. *What are your terms? What is it that you want?*

There was a sob in the boy's voice. "To be with my family."

Then that shall be our deal. You will not die. I will help you collect your family, and keep them together, forever. And in return, you will share your soul, your twice-seventh-born magic with me. You agree to this?

There was a pause, but I knew what Maghew would say. What he had said, all those years ago.

This was the story I had to change: the first one.

I focused. I claimed Maghew's body. His agony became my agony. I owned it all, the aching, the sorrow, the loneliness. The pain was a fire, burning in the core of me. I held his mouth shut. Maghew was trying to speak, to agree to the deal, but I would not let him.

The feeling of wrongness, strong as nausea, crashed through me. His story strained against me, trying to snap back, trying to reassert itself, trying to force Maghew's mouth open. I couldn't let that happen. I was trying to re-write the story, unravel it at the start. It chafed at my weakened will, at my paper-thin soul, trying to fix itself, trying to drag the boy back into his deal.

I kept his lips pressed together, struggling against the force of the past, strained tight as the leash of a rabid dog. But I was slipping away.

This was Maghew's story, not mine. I could not change it.

Yet Chloe had changed a story. I'd seen the evidence. Chloe said she held on long enough that the girl had felt her. Cordelia had known she wasn't alone.

I had to let Maghew know I was here.

So, fighting the sickness, the wrongness that reverberated down to my core. I spoke. It was hard to move Maghew's mouth, hard to get the word out. But I spoke to the voice that had lied to us all. The voice that told Maghew no one loved him. The voice that told Ollie we'd be better off without him. The voice that had told me not to invite my own brother to the library.

It came out as a hoarse shout, sharp as a shard of glass in my throat. "No!"

The room froze, the flickering candle suddenly impossibly steady. The pain was still there; the agony and heat of Maghew's body, but the story was no longer fighting me.

We'd stepped outside of the tale written in his book. Outside what had happened, hundreds of years ago, and into our own moment; two souls entwined at the end of our stories.

I held him there, in the space between him and the deal he'd made.

Silva. The girl from the library.

This wasn't the real Maghew, of course. He had died hundreds of years ago. But this was his soul, his memories, his life trapped in the pages of his book.

I spoke out loud, using Maghew's own mouth, his voice a wisp of sound.

"You're not alone," I said. "I'm here."

Please, do not leave me.

Maghew's desperation was bright as blood, and I understood. He shouldn't die alone. He needed family. He needed me, distant as I was. My own soul was draining out, and it was hard to focus.

"I'll stay," I said, using too much strength to move his dry lips. "I can't hold us here for long, but don't make the deal. Don't listen to the voice. It's lying."

No. The Whisper would not do that.

"It's been trying to drive a wedge between you and those who loved you."

No one loved me.

"Isabel loved you, so much. I was her. I felt it."

Silence. Maghew's abandonment had left him raw, his heartbreak echoing through hundreds of years.

"She wanted you to live with her. At her fiancé's estate."

There was a long pause.

Isabel wished for me to live with her?

"Yes. She thought the country air would be good for you. She wished she'd never left you that day ... this day. She wished she could go back and stay with you. Didn't you read her story?"

No ... I cannot. But she never returned.

"She thought the place you made for her was too dark for the light in your soul. She thought you had made a deal with something evil. And you did, didn't you?"

I was fading, my own life slipping away. I wanted to let go, to escape the pain of Maghew's body. I wanted to rest. But I knew once my grip on Maghew slipped, the story would start again.

"It's not too late. Please, don't make the deal. Let us all go."

I wished only to help, to give you all what you wanted. I wished for us to be together.

It was hard to move Maghew's mouth as I replied. The words were a weak whisper.

"It doesn't work like that. We can't make people stay, no matter how much we want to. They have to choose for themselves how their own story goes. All we can do is be there when they need us."

Tears slipped down my hot cheeks. I wasn't sure who was crying, him or me. His weak body was wracked with sobs, with the searing pain of the disease that was killing him and the ache of the battle in his head.

There was so little of me left, and I was so tired. I couldn't hold him anymore.

I let my grip slip, hoping it was enough.

The candle resumed its skittish flicker. Maghew exhaled as he took control of himself. He spoke, his voice rasping through his parched throat.

"I am so sorry. Thank you. Thank you. Forgive me."

The sweat was cold on Maghew's body. He trembled for a long while, and then fell still. His breathing grew weaker, bit by bit. His pulse slowed. Darkness crept in.

Maghew's chest grew still. The pain drifted away.

I was dying. Maghew was dying. Both of us.

The flickering candle was a pinprick of light in our rapidly shrinking world.

Maghew let go.

Chapter Twenty

I lay on my back on the floor of the magpie's library.

There was nothing left of me. The library had taken it all. I couldn't move. My chest was too heavy to rise and fall.

I was dying.

Dark clouds filled the sky on the other side of the glass dome. A flash of lightning illuminated the branches, casting shadows black as cracks in the walls. The angry rumble of thunder shook the books, still scattered in heaps on the floor, half-hidden by the gloom.

The letters around me lay as still as dead insects.

I wanted to inhale, to get oxygen into my lungs, but there was nothing to animate my body, it was all in my book. The air itself was a weight on my chest, suffocating me.

More lightning, shocking the branches into movement, like electricity through a corpse. They twisted, lurched, and pulled themselves away from the dark walls, winding back toward their own roots.

The weight on my chest shifted, just a little. I pulled a tiny gasp of air into my lungs.

Not enough. Blackness gathered at the edge of my vision.

Another flare of lightning, and the ear-splitting crash of thunder. The dome above me cracked. I wanted to lift an arm, to protect myself as the glass fell. I couldn't even flinch. But the shards melted away to nothing, dissolving in the air.

The pressure on me lifted, gram by gram. I pulled in a shallow breath. Then another.

My head spun.

The branches unraveled, unweaved, untangled. The books around me fluttered and crumbled, pages separating from spines that dissolved into the air as the paper faded to nothing. The text on the floor moved. It swirled up, forming a whirlwind of words, throwing themselves into the air, to the now-open sky. I struggled to sit up, pushing myself onto my elbows, and recoiled as I saw letters on my hand.

Silva would've noticed something was wrong sooner, if the magpie hadn't distracted her.

But the words weren't crowding this time, not forming a net on my skin. Instead they melted into my flesh. I lifted a hand to watch a line fade, glowing gold as it disappeared, spreading its light deep into my body

And yet, when she pushed against it, it swung open easily.

My story, returning to me. My memories, my feelings, my soul. I felt stronger as each letter slipped back into my skin. I sat up properly.

She wanted to tell Chloe about the library then. Shove it in her face, show her there was far more to reality, more to life than someone like her could ever imagine.

I pushed myself onto my knees. Watched the library twist into a tornado of letters and pages. Wind whipped my hair around, half-blinding me. I crawled away from it, struggling out of the spinning text, raising a hand to protect my face.

Another line settled on my arm.

As she turned the corner, her blood froze. The fire engine sat outside Grandpa's house.

I stumbled to my feet, feeling the life flow back into me. Shapes formed out of the words: figures, people. A girl of text, head back, eyes closed. A young boy written in the air, arms open to the sky above. They broke up, the letters spiraling out of the library to freedom. The wind sucked at me, tried to pull me into the growing funnel.

Lines from my book twisted out of the mass and returned to me.

On the cover a boy stood in an arcade, the familiar shape of him silhouetted against the light of the games.

I struggled against the hurricane of souls, arms wind-milling as I tried to get to the door, Maghew's door. My breath was sucked away by the storm. I faltered, slipped as the wind dragged me back.

I was weak, but more and more words landed on me.

She held Maghew's mouth shut, struggling against the force of the past.

I used the strength my story gave me. I pushed forward, fought toward the door. It swung open, pulled by the vortex behind me. It hung on its hinges, showing me the real library. The way back to my life.

I wanted my life, my stupid life, so much.

Pages whipped into my face, and I clawed at them, hurling them behind me. The wind tried to drag me back into the heart of the storm, tried to suck me away from my world.

I fell to my knees, ducked my head down to fight the pull. My nails dug into the cracks in the stone, aching as I wrenched myself forward. I screamed. The wind stole my cry, stole my breath as I crawled, inch by inch, toward freedom.

The metal of the door's hinges twisted like the branches of the library, and with a snap, the bottom one pulled away from the wall. I scrambled on as the other hinge broke, and the door swung toward me.

I ducked to one side and threw myself through.

The girl stayed with me. She was a different voice within my head, telling me a different story: a story where I was loved, a story where I was not alone.

As she spoke, as her words slipped into me, I let go. I let go of the tale I had been told for so long, where none would love me, where none but The Whisper would stay with me, where I must steal love, steal companionship, steal souls. I let go of the existence I had clung to, and the terrible cost of it.

I let go of The Whisper and began to unravel.

I had been dead for a long time. I had let The Whisper hold me together. Let it be the dark glue I used to catch souls, to stick them into my nest, to try to fill the holes in me.

I no longer had need of it.

The Whisper scrabbled to get back within me. It sought the gaps, murmuring, muttering, threatening.

You need me. You are nothing. I am all you have.

It was lying. It had always been lying. Why had I listened for so long? The only real power it had was the power I had given it: my magic. Without that, all it could do was whisper cruel lies in people's heads.

You were never loved. I am all you have.

It was just a voice. I had only to ignore it and listen to other voices that spoke to me, that had always spoken to me. Listen to Silva. To Isabel, to my brothers and sisters.

I had been much loved. Yet I had let The Whisper take that away, let it isolate me.

I exhaled, letting the souls coil out, away from me. Letting them free. They unthreaded, untangled, breaking apart my wings, my nest, my library. I fell apart, glad to feel it all slip away.

The Whisper raged, a dark storm whipping into a wild tempest. The souls streamed away from both of us. The girl fled to her own world, the living world, and my heart rejoiced to see her go. After a while, the anger of The Whisper burned itself out.

It gave up on me, and stillness returned.

Yet I was not alone. One other figure remained, made of almost-translucent letters. A sliver of a soul, trapped here nigh on as long as me. I fell to my knees.

"You ... you are still here."

"Of course. I missed thee, my dear Maghew."

"I am so sorry," I said, a sob swallowing my words. "I ... I ..."

She held her hand out to me. "I am sorry too. I should never have allowed thee to grow so alone, trapped in your dark room. I should never have left you, that day."

I reached for what was left of her soul with what was left of mine, still wondering that she could be here, afraid to blink in case I lost her again. Our fingers linked, and for a long time, we gazed upon each other. Then she tugged, pulling me to my feet with a grin that made my heart soar.

"Come, my little magpie. The others are waiting for us. 'Tis long past time for us to go."

Isabel and I left together.

Chapter Twenty-One

I landed on the floor of Hayling Library, one hand thrown out across the cold parquet. On my arm, the last of the text sunk into my skin.

I am so sorry. Thank you. Thank you. Forgive me.

I rubbed at the flesh where it disappeared, and it felt alive, pricking with sensation, tender with bruises. Wonderful, aching bruises that showed I was here, that proved I'd survived. Hot lines ran down my ankles where I'd scratched them, trying to claw off the words of Ollie's story.

I stood with ease, raked my tangled hair from my face with my fingers, twisted around, and saw the blank wall.

Maghew's door was gone. I ran my palms over the smooth surface to check. I felt the plaster, the paint, the normal wall under my fingers. I was free.

Ollie. I had to see Ollie. Had to find out if he was free, too.

I dashed for the entranceway. I shoved the door open and ran onto Elm Grove. The wind in my face was fantastic. My heart hammered in my chest and a stitch grew in my side, and I felt it all. The impact of each step reverberated through my body, jolting my bones, a beat that echoed through me: *alive, alive, alive*.

I sprinted all the way down Elm Grove and around the corner to Grandpa's cul-de-sac. I burst into the house.

"Ollie!"

He stood in the front room, cheeks flushed with color. "Silva!"

We ran to each other, and I hugged him, squeezing his skinny chest tight. I grabbed his shoulders and held him at arm's length, examining his face.

"Did it ...?" I was out of breath.

He grinned. "It was amazing. Light flowed back into me. What happened?"

"You're better?"

He nodded. "Back to how I was, at least."

I pulled him into another bear hug. "Oh, Ollie. Things will be different now. I promise. I'll be there for you. We'll get you help."

We stood like that as I caught my breath. He was still here. We were still alive, the both of us. Our stories unwritten. Ollie's tears were damp on my shoulder, but when we broke apart, he was smiling.

The pad of running feet on the driveway made us both turn, and a girl flashed past the window and into the hall. She stood in the doorway for a moment, staring at us.

It took a moment for me to recognize her, even with the white stripe in her hair.

"Chloe?" Her posture was different. She carried her limbs lightly, no longer stooped with their weight. Her eyes glistened with tears.

She lifted her arms, as if to show me how they'd changed. "Silva, what did you do?"

"I went into the magpie's story," I said. "I pulled him out."

Chloe's hand went to her mouth. She kept it there as I explained. Emotions flowed over her once-stony features, swift and smooth as water.

"Thank you," she said. "I never thought ..."

The slow creak of footsteps came down the stairs. Mum stopped a few steps from the bottom, eyes swollen with tears, hands tight on the bannister.

"You've been gone so long," she said.

Cold shot through me. "Sorry. Am I ... I mean, has he ..."

"Not yet, but ..." She took a deep breath. "We should all go up. Now."

She led the way to Grandpa's bedroom. The four of us shuffled in together and took our places around him.

His eyes were closed. The air was stale and the room almost silent, aside from the uncomfortable rattle of Grandpa's breath. Janet stood at the foot of the bed. She held a handful of scrunched tissues over her mouth.

I didn't need to peek into Janet's soul to know her story was a sad one. Her cousin and her husband both left her. Her mother died a lingering death as her daughter turned to stone. It was no wonder she was so lonely; no wonder she clung to my grandfather.

Grandpa shifted with a grunt. His eyes opened. I braced myself for the blank look I'd got back in the hospital, but he smiled. Lifted a hand in a small gesture toward his bedside table. "Want some?" His voice was hoarse, and the words seemed to be an effort.

A pack of Jelly Babies sat on the side.

He still knew me. I half-gasped, half-laughed, even as tears prickled at my eyes.

I was so glad to be his little girl one last time. "I'll always bite the heads off first, I promise."

Grandpa nodded. "They shouldn't have to suffer." He started coughing. A gasping, choking kind of cough that sounded like it might stop at any moment. I glanced at the others. Ollie's jaw clenched. Chloe clutched her hands together in front of her.

"You're all here," Grandpa said, in a wheezing whisper, once he got his breath back. "I'm so glad. This is what I wanted."

The room blurred with my tears.

"Oh, oh," Grandpa said. His shaking hand moved over his heart. "Peg. I never thought ..."

"It's okay," Mum murmured. "It's okay."

But he wasn't looking at her. He stared at the gap at the end of the bed, the space Mum and Janet had left between them. I followed his gaze. Hairs prickled at the back of my neck. For a second, I thought I saw the flicker

of text, twisting into the shape of a girl in a long night-
dress. I blinked and it was gone.

Grandpa smiled and nodded, as if he'd heard words
the rest of us couldn't catch.

"Yes," he said. "I'm coming. Just let me say goodbye."
Then he made an odd sound, like something had lodged
in his throat. An uncomfortable, wheezing sound.

Ollie grabbed my hand, and I squeezed his.

"No." Mum reached into her pocket, fumbled for her
phone. "No. I can't let this happen. I don't care what I
said. I'm calling an ambulance."

Grandpa caught my gaze then, as the effort to breathe
shook his frail body. There was no confusion, no panic
in his eyes. He moved his head: a slight shake.

My heart clenched. I didn't want to let this happen,
either. But it wasn't up to me.

I took my mother's wrist, gently moving her fingers
away from her phone.

"Mum, it's time."

She turned to Ollie and I, tears streaming down her
cheeks. Then Grandpa started breathing again, and everyone leaned back, relieved that the moment had been
postponed.

In the end, Grandpa's death wasn't like the deaths on
telly. There it was obvious and quick; the dying person
muttered meaningful last words, their eyes closed, and
the monitoring machine flat-lined with a dramatic whine.

Grandpa didn't have a heart machine, of course. And there was time with us. Time to cry, time to hug him, and each other. Time for us to get tired from all the standing. Time to sit on the edge of his bed and stroke his legs under his sheets. Time to offer him sips of water through a straw, and for Mum to give him more pain-killers. Time to tell him we loved him so many times that I was sure he was getting sick of hearing it.

He told us he loved us too. Hours passed as he sunk deeper into his pillows. As the afternoon slid toward evening, his breathing got worse, until it was painful to hear it, until I felt as if I were choking too. Grandpa grew tired, his eyes opening and closing, falling into and out of sleep.

When his eyes closed for the last time, he muttered something I couldn't quite hear. But it sounded like "she's waiting."

He stopped breathing, for almost a minute. I felt as if I was collapsing from the inside, as if my heart were caving in. But just when I gave up hope, he inhaled, air gently lifting his chest, before halting again. It happened twice more, for longer each time, and then he took a final, faltering breath.

We were quiet for about ten minutes after the last wheeze, waiting, but no more came.

I squeezed my eyes shut, as sorrow crested in me, a wave of pain taking my breath. I bit my lip and listened to the hiss of the sea. In. Out. The whisper of the tide filled the room, taking up the space left by Grandpa's stopped breath.

It wasn't a happy ending, but it was the right one for Grandpa.

The doctor came and went, and the undertaker took Grandpa away. I couldn't bear to watch him be wheeled out of the house where he belonged. The grief was a hot knot in my chest. But the ache felt right, it felt real, it was a part of being alive, of being whole.

Janet and Chloe went home as it got late, Chloe and me hugging tight as she left. Janet paused for a moment at the door, as if she wanted to say something to Mum, but she shook her head, and turned away without speaking.

After I got into my pajamas, I drifted back into Grandpa's room, and found myself by his empty bed, staring at the Jelly Babies on the side table. The air still smelled of him: musty aftershave and digestive biscuits. But he belonged to the past now, just like Maghew, just like Isabel and Margaret.

It didn't seem real.

I wandered over to his cupboards, opened the doors, and ran my hand along the sleeves of shirts he'd never fill again. I went to the bed and picked up Margaret's doll.

I'd give it to Chloe, just as he'd promised.

Something caught my eye, under the pillow. I lifted it, and found a small pile of pictures, some in frames, some loose, a few with sticky corners still on them, as if they'd been pulled out of photo albums. There was Grandpa as a boy with Margaret and his mother, and Mum holding me as a baby. There were others of Ollie and Chloe, and a few of people who were probably distant relatives.

Grandpa must have taken them from the shelves, from photo albums, and from the fridge, and kept them under his pillow. He'd been afraid of forgetting us, so he'd kept us all close, safe in his bed.

Just like Maghew and his mementos.

I sat on the bed then, clutching the pictures. Grandpa was afraid of losing his memories. They were all he had of his sister, his parents, his wife; that's why they were so important to him. That's why he couldn't bear to live without them.

I couldn't make Grandpa stay, but he'd left me a treasure trove of memories of him: my own collection, a library filled with happy stories that I could visit whenever I wanted.

Mum entered the room. She was silent for a long moment and gave a little cough before she spoke. "Ollie had a talk with me. He told me how he'd been feeling, and that you thought he might be depressed. I've made him an appointment in Manchester, to speak to a doctor."

I spun around. "We're still moving to Manchester? What about the funeral?"

"We'll come back for that. It won't be for a couple

of weeks. Work needs me to start on the new contract before then."

"But can't … can't we move here? It's your house now, right? If we don't have to pay rent, can't you get a lower-paying job and stay?"

Mum looked out of Grandpa's window. "Silva, I have to put this house on the market."

Cold cracked open inside me. "No. Mum, please …"

"I'm sorry. My job needs me to move around. I don't expect you to understand."

But I did. It all clicked into place.

Her job didn't need her to move around, that was backwards. She'd needed a job that moved around. She couldn't stay in one place. She was afraid to.

Don't say it. You're wrong. She'll think you're crazy.

That voice again. Of course it wasn't gone. It had used Maghew's magic, but it existed long before he was born. It would always be there, muttering in people's minds. The library wasn't its only trap, the only way it kept people apart.

It hissed in our heads. It told us that we were alone, that other people wouldn't understand. It told Maghew he wasn't loved. It told Ollie that things would never get better, that his own family would be better off without him. It tried to drown out the real world and isolate us in the numbing fog of its lies.

I was done listening.

I flicked back through the photos, until I found an

old one of Janet. It was grainy, and she wore different clothes, but now I knew what I was looking for it was easy to recognize the big hair, the blue eyeshadow.

"The magpie's door is gone, Mum. It won't follow you anymore."

Her gaze snapped back from the window and her mouth fell open. She stared for a moment, and then pulled herself together. "I'm sorry. What did you say?"

Maghew had been showing me my own relatives, trying to bring us together. In the family tree of the library, my story and Ollie's were right above another book, with a girl in a borrowed silver dress.

"It was a cinema, wasn't it?" I said. "Janet went to see a horror film with Uncle Tom. You followed the magpie and found the door."

Mum wobbled for a moment and sat on Grandpa's bed.

"How ... how did you know? How could you know?"

"What happened to you? In the film?"

Her fingers went to her mouth. "It ... it wasn't a film. I was there. Actually there. Living it. It was terrifying. Violent and painful, a boy running from wolves. I felt it all. The fear. The agony of his bleeding feet as he scrabbled over stone." She exhaled. "After that, I kept seeing the door, but no one else could. I was so scared of it."

"It's okay, Mum."

Her voice shook. "They ... shut down the Hayling cinema. It reappeared at the video shop. I moved away and it followed. But if I kept moving, it took a while to find me. I thought I was …"

I sat on the bed next to Mum. Put my arm around her shoulders. "Shh. It's over."

She kept talking, the words rushing out of her in a torrent.

"I met your father, and the door disappeared. I thought I was better. I had you and Ollie, but things got tough. Your dad and I fought a lot. It … it came back." Mum bit her lip. "I asked work for a relocation. Your father didn't want to move, and I couldn't tell him about the door. He made me choose: my job or him."

"The door is gone. I promise."

She faced me. "You saw it? Oh Silva, you didn't go in, did you?"

I called Ollie and we explained it all. Mum wept. She told us of the static that had flickered over her skin while she'd been watching Grandpa that morning. The static that had made her feel just a little better, in spite of her sorrow.

She hugged us tight. The three of us talked together, long into the night. We talked about the magpie's trap. We talked about the distances we'd let grow between us, the whispers we'd listened to, the secrets that kept us apart.

We'd been such idiots. We'd isolated ourselves from each other, escaped into separate worlds long before I found the library. Mum's job, my books, Ollie's games.

We cried over the time we'd wasted, with each other, and with Grandpa.

Finally, we talked about the future, and what it could look like for us.

Chapter Twenty-Two

There was no magpie on the lawn as we pulled into the driveway six weeks later.

"Why is the front door open?" Ollie asked.

I peered through the gap between Mum and the boxes on the passenger seat; through the drizzle smeared across the windscreen by the wipers. Christmas lights glinted in the hall. Janet and Chloe appeared, hurrying out toward the car as Mum yanked on the handbrake.

"Because they were waiting for us," I said. "Standing back a bit, so they didn't get wet."

Chloe waved like a maniac. "Silva! Ollie!" She'd dyed her hair pink. It brightened her whole face.

I opened the door, desperate to stretch my legs after the long journey crammed in with all our stuff, but Chloe pounced on me before I had a chance, yanking me into a bear hug.

"That suits you," I said, pointing at her hair when she let go. She grinned, and bent down to stroke Tonic, who purred as she rubbed against my legs. She sauntered past us both, tail up, into Grandpa's house.

No, into our home. I'd have to get used to that.

Janet bobbed forward, arms out, leaning in for a hug as Mum stood and got out of the car. Mum reacted too slowly, probably still stiff from the drive.

Janet's face fell, and she stepped back, awkwardly. "We decorated the house, like we used to for Uncle Chris. But perhaps we shouldn't have. I mean, I know it's your place now; Chloe and I just thought …"

"It's wonderful. Come here." Mum grabbed her cousin, pulling her into a tight hug.

There was a lot for us to deal with. Mum had endured decades of nightmares; had spent most of her life running. Chloe had to recover after five years of being turned to stone. Ollie would need professional help for the foreseeable future, and we'd all be mourning Grandpa for years. The grief was a raw wound, a hole in my chest that still took my breath when I thought of him. The funeral had been hard on all of us.

But in the weeks since, Ollie's smile had peeked out a little more.

There would be bad days as well as good. The voice would keep talking to us, trying to keep us apart. We'd have to learn how to listen to each other, instead of it.

It wouldn't be easy, but together, we could heal.

Over Mum's shoulder, I saw Janet's eyes fill with tears. She clutched at Mum as if she were a life belt. They didn't let go for a long time.

I wondered how many other families were suffering. How many people were barely holding on, listening to the lies whispered in their heads. I wished I could talk to them. I wished I could tell them they weren't alone. That they were loved, more fiercely and deeply than they could imagine.

Mum and Janet broke apart, but Mum kept her hand around her cousin's shoulders. They stepped up into the house together, Janet wiping at her eyes. Chloe followed.

Ollie glanced back at me. "Come on, sis." He held out his hand.

In front of him, the hall glittered with lights and tinsel. I took Ollie's hand, and we stepped into our new home.

This was the story I wanted. The story of us. We'd write it together.

I was excited to see what would happen next.

Acknowledgements

Writing books is not a solitary pursuit. In fact, one of the best things about it is the community. I am lucky to have an amazing network of friends and professionals in my corner, all of whom make the process go better at every step of the way.

As always, major thanks to Barry Jowett, my publisher and editor, as well as the other lovely people at DCB and Cormorant, particularly Marc Côté. A special thank you to Emma Dolan for the wonderful cover, which I still can't stop staring at.

Thanks to The Rights Factory. My fab agent and friend Lydia Möed was enthusiastic about this slightly odd story from the start, and I will miss working with her — but I am very grateful to Ali McDonald for taking this book on.

I am indebted to the Ontario Arts Council for their support. They help make writing time possible for so many of us.

Thanks also go to the Humber School for Writers and to my mentor, Tim Wynne Jones, whose wonderful insights helped me solve many problems in early drafts of this book, and let me see what was possible.

Thank you so, so much to everyone who read this book and gave me feedback through what felt like endless drafts: James Bow, Megan Crewe, Shalini Nanayakkara, Angela Misri, Claudia Osmond, Nicole Winters, Helaine Becker, Leah Bobet (whose encouragement came at the most necessary time), Ann Marie Meyers, Jocelyn Geddie and Jo Hope.

I read all of your comments so many times, and it often felt like you were talking to me when I rewrote. On the hardest days everything felt more possible with your voices guiding me with helpful feedback. Thank you so much for being the kind thoughts whispering in my head.

And thank you, most of all, to my family — both here and on Hayling. We might not all be together, but you're always there for me, when I need it most.

Kate Blair is a native of Hayling Island, UK, and is now a Canadian citizen living in Toronto. She has written two novels for young adults. The first, *Transferral*, was a finalist for the Manitoba Young Readers' Choice Award and the Saskatchewan Young Readers' Choice Snow Willow Award, was longlisted for the Sunburst Award, and was a Canadian Children's Book Centre *Best Books for Kids and Teens* Starred Selection. Her second novel, *Tangled Planet*, was also longlisted for the Sunburst Award, and received a Starred Review from *School Library Journal*. *The Magpie's Library* is Blair's first novel for middle-grade readers.